Revenge

A novel by

Stevie Turner

Revenge
Copyright Stevie Turner 2015
All Rights Reserved

Although some place names are real, all characters' names and the characters themselves are fictitious. Any similarity to persons living or deceased is purely coincidental.

Dedication

Dedicated to all those who should have known better.

Acknowledgements

Thanks to Obsessed by Books Designs for the cover. Thanks also to Michael and Kate for their constructive comments on how to improve the book.

Table of Contents

SYNOPSIS:

Teacher Alistair Veale is just coasting along in his 20 year marriage to Ann. His two sons Tom and Jake are growing up fast and have their own interests, but he still enjoys a close relationship with 13-year-old daughter Jessie, his 'Princess'.

When Alistair takes 14 children from his tutor group on a week-long school trip to the Isle of Wight, a new Science teacher, Carly Jessop, goes along to keep an eye on the 6 girls. Alistair notices a growing attraction between himself and Carly, which cannot be ignored.

However, when Alistair and Carly begin an affair the consequences are horrific and far-reaching, threatening not only Alistair's livelihood, but also his peace of mind and the relationship he has with his own three children.

CHAPTER 1

"DENBIGH, YOU'RE OUT!"

"But, sir!" Jack Denbigh stood defiantly, with hands on hips.

"No buts; out! You were caught fair and square by Pritchard!" Alistair Veale indicated a thumb towards the bench.

Muttering under his breath, Denbigh turned away; scuffing his trainers along the ground and slumping down onto the bench. Alistair looked over his shoulder and grinned to himself at the sight of Jack's moody face; the boy had a lot to learn about fair play and gamesmanship.

"Come on Tucker; whack that ball! Fielders, go back a bit!" Alistair signalled to the Braithwaite brothers as sixteen stone Leon Tucker picked up his bat.

"It's alright Sir; he can hit the ball but he can't run to save his life!" Rick Braithwaite shouted from the other end of the rounders' green.

"Shut up, *prick*." Leon's bass tones echoed around the pitch as he adopted a batting stance.

"Leon *fucker*." Rick Braithwaite mouthed the last word after a quick glance at Alistair's expression.

"If you two have finished hurling insults at each other, then let's get on with the game! We've only got another ten minutes." Alistair checked his watch, looking forward to two rounds of ham and tomato sandwiches and a cup of coffee in the staff room.

True to form, Leon's massive arms aided the ball's poetic-like flight over the roof of the gym and into the next field. Alistair cheered, as Tucker, to his eternal delight, lumbered around the four posts with the agility of a three-legged elephant, but somehow managed to return to the batting square seconds in front of Ben Braithwaite's throw to the backstop.

"Well done Tucker!" Alistair believed in giving praise where it was due. "We'll carry on tomorrow lunchtime as usual. Who's keeping score?" He blew a whistle to mark the end of the game.

"Denbigh." Will Patterson grinned as he collected up the bats. "At least that's what I *think* he's writing in his notebook."

"I'll keep it up here anyway." Alistair tapped his forehead. "Bring me back the sports cupboard key after registration."

"Okay, Sir."

Stomach growling with hunger, Alistair made his way to the staff room. Most of the armchairs were taken already, but he spied one unoccupied chair in a corner next to the fridge. The kettle still felt hot, and he set it to boil briefly while grabbing a clean mug from the draining board and adding a spoonful of coffee.

"Did they run off all that hormonal energy?"

Smiling, Carly Jessop made her way over to where he stood, and poured the dregs of her cup of tea down the sink.

"Yeah, I think so. It's always better in the afternoons if we can have a little game of rounders at lunchtime." He chuckled whilst secretly admiring the way her thick red hair curled around her face. "I like getting out in the fresh air anyway."

"Shall I be Mum?" Carly held out his cup.

"Sure; thanks. No sugar."

Careful not to appear to be staring too hard at the school's striking new science teacher, Alistair bent down and opened the fridge, taking out Ann's carefully prepared lunchbox.

"Thanks for the coffee." He took the cup from her hand, noting the absence of any engagement or wedding rings.

"That's okay. I'll leave you to eat in peace; I've got some marking to do before registration."

He watched her retreating back as he devoured the first sandwich, noting with appreciation how the tight skirt she wore accentuated her body's curves.

"Penny for your thoughts, but then I'm not sure I want to know them anyway!" Maisie Brooks followed his line of vision and laughed.

"Just planning for this afternoon." Alistair was thankful he had stopped blushing thirty years earlier.

"Listen Ali; I can't go on the Shanklin trip. The hospital have called me in for a hysterectomy at last. I've told Leonard about it; he's going to ask around to see who else can go."

"Sorry to hear that; Ann had the same thing done last

year. I remember she couldn't lift anything for about six weeks." Alistair nodded in sympathy.

"I was looking forward to the trip; so sorry." Maisie shrugged. "I have to go in at the beginning of July."

"Don't be silly. Your health comes before any job." Alistair picked up another sandwich and bit into it.

"That's what my old man says, but I still feel guilty, leaving you in the lurch."

"Leonard will find somebody, don't worry."

At 1.45 Alistair washed up his mug and made his way back to the classroom for afternoon registration. He could see the more conscientious students in his tutor group already settled and revising for their upcoming GCSE's, but the usual three were arsing about as usual at the back.

"Sanderson, Tucker and Denbigh, please take your seats." He opened up the register, on alert for any backchat.

"Sir; Pritchard didn't catch me out, he dropped the ball and then picked it up again quickly." Jack Denbigh's affronted voice permeated around the room. "He's admitted it."

"Only because you most likely offered him a bog brushing if he didn't." Alistair laughed along with the rest of the group. "You forget I was standing there as well. Patterson, where's that key?"

"Here, Sir." Will Patterson came to the front desk.

"Thanks. Kylie, please could you turn around and stop chatting to Lisa. Now, let's hope nobody's skived off this afternoon." He picked up his pen and called out the first name on the register.

CHAPTER 2

HE PREFERRED TO mark books alone in the classroom at the end of the day. In that way he could keep his work life separate, and could devote the rest of the evening to Ann and the children. In the early days of their marriage he remembered how Ann would look over his shoulder as he read and corrected English essays, and then worm herself onto his lap; her resentment almost palpable at not being the centre of his attention. He would then have to read quicker and less professionally; perhaps missing an incorrect spelling or a grammatical error. Within a year it had become usual for him to arrive home at half past five, but with the marking completed along with plans for the next day's lesson. After 18 years it was part of his normal routine.

When the last of the Year 10's had drifted out, Alistair sat back at his desk with a sigh, took off his glasses, rubbed his eyes, and ran a hand through his thick brown hair. The end of a long summer term was in sight, and the delicious six week break stretched before him just tantalisingly out of reach. He replaced the rimless frames once again, yawned, and opened the first book for marking just as the classroom door opened.

"I left my cardigan in my desk, Sir. My mum'll go mad if I don't bring it home."

He looked up from Gerald Smithson's badly spelt essay to see one of his tutor group girls, Adrienne Draper, hurrying into the room.

"Hurry then Adrienne, you'll miss the bus." He smiled at the quiet, unassuming schoolgirl.

"I let Gillian know to tell them to wait." Adrienne collected her cardigan and walked towards his desk. "Are you looking forward to the Shanklin trip, Sir?"

"Yes, the Isle of Wight is a lovely island; you'll see. Have you ever been there?" He hid his impatience to recommence marking.

"Never; do I need a passport?" Adrienne looked at him questioningly.

"No, it's part of England." He resisted the urge to grin. "You won't be in a foreign land."

"Oh good. My mum hates going abroad." Adrienne waved as she turned towards the door. "See you tomorrow, Sir."

"Yes, see you tomorrow, Adrienne."

He waited until she was gone to laugh out loud.

There were still a few vehicles left in the staff car park at five o'clock. He decided his silver Mondeo did not look too out of place amongst the Fiestas and Mini Coopers as he strode towards it. A thick blanket of warmth exuded from inside the car as he opened the door, and he decided to start the engine, turn on the air-conditioning, and wait outside for a moment to let the interior cool down. While he stood absent-mindedly watching shimmering waves of heat bouncing off the roof of his car, he was suddenly aware that somebody was opening a door behind him.

"Lucky old you with the air-con!"

He glanced over his shoulder to see Carly Jessop unlocking a beat-up looking red Micra.

"Yeah; it's what you get for being Head of English. I'm holding out for a Range Rover next term." He smiled at her. "You'll be lucky!" She laughed. "Oh, by the way, Leonard asked me if I'd be willing to take Maisie's place on the Shanklin trip, so I said yes. I thought I'd better show willing in my first year."

"Welcome on board." He felt strangely uplifted at hearing her remark. "Six o'clock start next Monday morning then in the car park here."

"Joy." Carly grinned as she closed the driver's door and started the engine.

The end-of-term tiredness had evaporated by the time he brought the Mondeo to rest on his driveway. As he stepped out of the car he could hear Tom and Jake kicking a football about in the back garden. The side gate was swinging open and he walked down the path, catching the ball deftly as it flew towards him, aided in its flight by a hefty kick from his son's size ten boot:

"Hey Dad!" Tom came running up to him with hands outstretched.

"Hi! Careful with this." He handed the ball back to his son. "You really need to go down on the green. This garden's not big enough."

"Mum told us dinner was nearly ready."

"So you're hovering about like a pair of locusts, eh?"

"Yeah, something like that." Tom grinned.

"Hi Dad! My bike's got a puncture." Fifteen-year-old Jake waved to Alistair.

"I showed you how to mend it last time."

"I forgot."

"After dinner then." Alistair smiled at his son and opened the conservatory door.

"Okay."

"Hi darling." Ann Veale laid knives and forks down on the dining room table and came through the open sliding door towards him.

"Hey." He smiled and kissed her. "Good day?" "Great!"

Ann smiled at him. "I've been told today that I've got the lunchtime supervisor job at St. Luke's, starting in September. There might even be a chance for me to become a teaching assistant in the future."

"That's marvellous!" He put his arms around her. "I promise I never said a word in your favour."

"Yuk; put a stop to it Dad." Jake hung around the dinner table. "I'm starving."

"I'm just kissing your mother. It's allowed; we're married." Alistair broke away from his wife and ruffled the top of his son's head. "Can I help with dinner?"

"No, just call Tom in and get both of them to wash their hands."

"Where's Jessie?" He glanced quickly into the dining room.

"Upstairs; sulking again probably." Ann rolled her eyes. "I think the hormones have kicked in."

"Oh God, no. I'll just nip up and see her."

He read the latest note on the bedroom door informing him that no boys were allowed to enter, and grinned. Alistair could hear music from an unidentifiable boyband coming from within. He knocked softly.

"Hi Jessie! Dinner's nearly ready!"

The door flew open and he was suddenly enveloped in a whirl of long silky brown hair, while two limpet-like arms clung tenaciously around his neck. He swung his thirteen year old daughter around and around on the landing.

"Daddy! I didn't know you were home!" Jessie Veale shrieked in his ear. "Mr Williams gave me an A plus for my essay today!"

"That's wonderful!" He laughed and kissed her cheek. "Come on downstairs now and tell me all about it."

"Okay."

As he followed Jessie downstairs he marvelled at the speed of his daughter's mood swings. *How could anyone change from petulant to pleasant in such a short space of time?* He vowed to investigate female child development a bit further on Google.

CHAPTER 3

HE SPRUNG OUT of bed at 5am on Sunday 6th July, the morning of the trip. The school's minibus sitting on his driveway was already packed with possessions, and happily, as far as he could tell from looking out of the window, it promised to be a fine day.

"Why have you got to go so early?" Ann, yawning, sat up in bed and looked at him.

"It's a four hour trip down to Portsmouth to get the ferry, possibly longer with stops. One or other of the girls are bound to need the loo every five minutes."

"That statement just shows how you still don't understand women even after twenty years of marriage." Ann yawned again. "We go to the loo when the chance arises, whether we need to go or not."

"I'll drive fast and bypass the service stations, so there's no opportunity." Alistair rolled his eyes.

"What about periods? If the girls have periods they'll need to stop."

"Oh God, I'll leave that to Carly." He could have bitten

out his tongue as soon as he had said her name.

"Carly? You're going with Carly?" Ann was wide awake now. "Where's Maisie? Why didn't you tell me Carly was going?"

"Maisie had a hysterectomy last Thursday. I forgot to tell you." He hoped she would believe the lie. "I'm just going to have a shower and then I'll be off. Go back to sleep, darling. Sorry to wake you up."

Ann, deflated, lay back on her pillow.

"She's beautiful; I saw her at Jake's parents' evening."

"So?" Alistair tried to appear nonchalant as he collected clean clothes from his wardrobe.

"*So*…..you'll be with her for a whole week."

"Look." He came and sat down on her side of the bed and pointed to his wedding ring. "Have I ever strayed in the twenty years that we've been married?"

"Not as far as I know." Ann's voice sounded as sulky as Jessie's on a bad day.

"Well then, you'll just have to trust me won't you? Anyway, there'll be fourteen teenagers to look after. That'll stop us having sex if nothing else." He laughed. "You've nothing to worry about, I promise." He kissed her and stood up.

"Sorry, it's just that she's extremely pretty and younger than me." Ann sighed. "I promise I won't mention it again."

"Go back to sleep. I'll see you on Friday evening."

He saw her already waiting there in the car park and sitting on a large rucksack, as he steered the minibus in through the school gates at 05:50. Her red hair shone in the early morning sunshine, and what he could see of her legs in her knee-length shorts appeared muscular and slightly tanned.

Alistair, his manhood already beginning to stiffen, tore his gaze away from Carly's attributes and concentrated on parking the bus. As he turned off the engine and opened up the doors, she stood and grabbed her rucksack and walked over to him.

"Hi Ali; I thought you weren't coming!" She laughed and climbed into the front seat, stowing her rucksack in the foot well.

"I said six, not five o'clock. How long have you been sitting there?" He grinned at her and stretched.

"Oh, not long. Barry dropped me off on the way to the gym. With a bit of luck he'll pick me up on Friday too."

He felt a sinking sensation in the pit of his stomach, but was not sure whether it was due to hunger, or the fact that she had mentioned the existence of a partner. Alistair kept a fixed smile on his face as he brushed away mental images of her lying on top of a faceless muscle-bound hulk. As the first car came through the gates he waved and climbed out of the bus.

"Oh-oh; here comes Denbigh. His mother probably couldn't wait to get rid of him."

"He always listens very carefully at my Sex and Relationship classes." Carly giggled. "In fact during the whole lesson you can even hear a pin drop."

"He probably knows more than you do." Alistair replied dryly. "I dread the thought of Denbigh let loose on the female population."

Several parents then arrived at the same time with their children, keeping Alistair busy stowing luggage and Carly sorting out seating arrangements and attempting to prise a tearful Celie Ingram away from her mother.

"Sir, is Celie going to cry for the whole week?"   Kevin

Sanderson sighed as he climbed on board the bus. "She gets travel sick as well. She puked up in the coach on the way to that museum last year."

"Hopefully no on both counts, but let her sit at the front next to Miss Jessop." Alistair could have kicked himself again for not bringing a suitable receptacle.

"Sir, Tucker's taking up a whole seat to himself and there aren't any more left." Oliver Stewart whined.

"Move him along with your boot." Alistair stopped the corners of his mouth from turning upwards as he locked the back doors securely.

"Leon, please move towards the window and let Oliver sit down." Carly climbed on the bus and gave the offending boy who was twice her size, a hard glare.

"His arse is too big." Robert Evans shook his head. "He can't help it; his mum makes him eat whole cows out of the fridge."

"Shut it, Evans." Leon shifted up unwillingly. "At least I'm not *ginger.*"

"Robert, don't be uncharitable. Leon, I hope you are not referring to myself with that remark." Carly's voice was cold, but with the hint of a smile.

"Or me." Keira Trelawny, aloof and hauntingly beautiful, tossed her waist length red locks, and fixed Leon with an evil eye.

"No, Miss. Sorry Keira, I meant Evans, Miss. His hair's redder." Leon blushed and looked out of the window.

"Right; if everybody's here, then we'll get going." Carly manoeuvred herself into the front seat. "If anyone feels sick, then let me know."

"I feel sick, Miss." Celie Ingram blew her nose.

"That's just nerves, Celie. Mr Veale's only just started up the engine."

CHAPTER 4

"CAN WE HAVE some music, Sir?" Kylie Morris shouted from somewhere near the back of the bus. "I forgot to bring my iPod."

"Yeah, any rap?" Tyler Marshall beat out a rhythm on the back of the seat in front with his hands. "Dr Dre; Jay-Z?"

Alistair, negotiating the busy roundabout at Ipswich leading onto the A12, could not think of anything worse.

"Try again, Marshall. If I have to listen to that I'll end up driving into the wall. I can just about tolerate Radio One though. Miss Jessop, can you find something suitable?" Alistair turned briefly to smile at Carly.

"Radio One it is." Carly shouted as she switched on the radio, before muttering under her breath. "Although I prefer Classic FM."

"Ah, now you're talking; so do I." Alistair kept his voice low and nodded.

"Miss, I need the loo." Celie Ingram looked up at Carly anxiously.

"Really? So soon?"

"Yeah, sorry." Celie nodded to confirm her distress.

"Okay, we'll stop at the next garage. Who else needs the toilet?" Carly looked around at the raised hands. "Is that all the girls?"

"Yeah!" Lisa Lambert's strident tones echoed around the bus.

"How much longer is it 'till we get to the ferry?" Michael Pritchard enquired hopefully.

"About another three hours, Pritchard." Alistair sighed as he signalled left at the sight of a service station "Not counting wee stops along the way."

As the end of the journey came in sight, with a great deal of relief Alistair turned off the radio and handed the ferry ticket to one of the Wightlink crew through the open driver's window.

"Lane nine. You've missed the eleven o'clock. Next one's in a quarter of an hour at eleven thirty."

"Sorry, Miss. I couldn't help it." Celie looked crestfallen. "I feel okay now though."

"That's alright. You gave us enough warning." Carly smiled and knelt up on the seat to face the back as the bus came to a halt in the queue. "There's loos over there for anyone who's desperate, but it's best to stay on the bus if you can." She pointed a finger in the right direction. "We haven't got a lot of time until the next ferry, but once we get on board there'll be food, drinks and toilets."

"I'm hungry." Leon Tucker complained.

"Gnaw on your arm." Robert Evans snorted.

"Drop dead." Leon looked over his shoulder towards the seat behind.

Alistair, covertly watching the back of the bus through

the rear view mirror, suddenly noticed that Kevin had changed places with Gillian Lister, and was now sitting rather too close to Lisa, who was gazing at him with eyes resembling those of a surprised doe.

"Miss, I don't want to sit next to Freddie." Gillian complained bitterly.

"Sanderson; get back in your seat, please." Alistair turned to face the back. "The seating plan stays the same throughout the trip."

"Why?" Kevin Sanderson *tutted* with annoyance.

"Girls on one side, boys on the other; that's how it is." Alistair's face remained expressionless as he remembered his own fifteen year old raging hormones.

"That sucks." Kevin placed a well-aimed kick at Freddie Peterson's shin as he sat back in his place.

"Ah; they're waving us on the ferry now." Alistair started up the engine. "Seat belts back on please."

Making sure there was nobody lagging behind, Alistair followed Kevin Sanderson up several steep flights of steps from the car deck to the passenger area. Carly's light perfume wafted pleasantly on the air, and he watched her red curls bouncing along at the head of a line of excited teenagers.

"We'll claim these seats around here." He indicated an area with his right hand. "There's toilets either side of the café that you can see over there. Don't get lost or wander off onto the upper decks. You can queue up for sandwiches and drinks if you're hungry, and the crossing will take about forty minutes. There will be lunch at the hotel when we arrive if you want to save your money."

"I'm on a diet." Keira Trelawny flopped down on a seat,

looked out of the window, and waved towards some low-rise flats where people sat on their balconies idly passing the time.

"I'm not." Leon Tucker quickly joined the head of the queue for sandwiches.

"Hey! That guy in the yellow shorts waved to me!" Keira signalled rather more energetically.

"We're moving, Sir." Adrienne Draper sat on her hands and grinned. "I hope it's not going to be choppy."

"It's not the open sea as such, Adrienne, it's the Solent. The crossing is usually smooth." Alistair replied, keeping one eye on Denbigh, Pritchard and Evans as they made their way to the sandwich queue.

"I'm going to get a coffee. Do you want one?" Carly glanced at Alistair and rummaged in her purse.

"Sure, thanks. Here; my round." He opened his wallet and gave her five pounds.

"Cheers; I'll get the next lot." Carly stood up. "Tucker, are you really going to eat all that?"

"Yes Miss; it'll keep me going 'till lunch." Leon sat down with a laden tray. "This is only elevenses."

"Where's Sanderson and Lisa?" Alistair looked around. "Has anybody seen them?"

"They're necking round the other side of the café." Leon bit into a giant sausage roll.

"Not for long they won't be." Alistair sighed and got to his feet. "I'll soon put a stop to that."

CHAPTER 5

"WHERE ARE YOU sleeping Sir, in with Miss?"

Alistair could not think of anything nicer at that particular moment. However, he ignored several suppressed giggles and nudges, and used the sly advantage of an extra two inches in his six foot one frame in a poor attempt to tower over Kevin Sanderson.

"Miss Jessop will slumber unmolested downstairs on the second floor with the girls, and you lot, for your sins, have got me up here with you. Whilst your suggestion conjures up very pleasurable mental imagery, I much prefer the stink of unwashed feet and bowel gas that seems to be already so pervasive here along the boys' corridor, although luckily I have the room next door." Alistair wrinkled his nose. "Is that you, Evans?"

"It's Tucker, Sir; it's all that white bread he ate on the ferry." Robert Evans wafted a hand in front of his nose.

"The one who smelt it, dealt it." Leon settled back on his bed with a packet of crisps.

"Cheers for that, Tucker. Now that lunch is over with, if

you've all unpacked your things, then we can go down on the beach. I'll meet you all downstairs in the foyer in fifteen minutes. Those who want to go in the sea must be proficient at swimming. Our first trip out tomorrow will be to Osborne House at East Cowes."

"Who lives there Sir?" Freddie Peterson's voice piped up through the open door of the room opposite.

"Nobody now; it was Queen Victoria and Prince Albert's summer home in the eighteen hundreds." Alistair could only stand and gape in awe at the depth of Peterson's ignorance.

"Blimey; it must be falling down then." Freddie threw his swimming trunks to land on Oliver Stewart's head.

Happy to be out of Tucker, Sanderson and Evans' stuffy room, Alistair made his way down to the second floor. The girls were flitting about in the corridor, and he smiled at Carly standing in the doorway of the bedroom nearest to him.

"Beach trip then? Everyone ready?" He noticed her flimsy sundress with approval. "I've told the boys to meet me down in the foyer in a quarter of an hour."

"I'll come and wait with you and let the girls get on with it." Carly swung her beach bag over her shoulder.

Following her downstairs, Alistair smelt the sweet aroma of a fresh application of perfume. He found an armchair, faced it towards the stairs, and brought another matching chair towards it. He sank down and sighed, glad of the temporary lull.

"I'll be knackered by the end of the week, keeping that lot under control."

"At least you haven't got to deal with homesickness. Celie Ingram can cry for England." Carly rolled her eyes and slumped down into her armchair.

"Leon Tucker exudes as much methane as a whole field of cows if that's any consolation." Alistair grinned and looked past the reception desk. "I'll be propping up that bar over there tonight when my lot are in bed."

"I'll be joining you, just after I've ensured that Lisa hasn't crept up the stairs." A faint smile played upon Carly's lips.

"And check that Sanderson hasn't sneaked downstairs as well while you're at it." Alistair laughed. "When I was fifteen I would have managed it somehow."

"God; when I was that age I was so shy I couldn't even speak to a boy without blushing, let alone anything else." Carly sighed. "They sure do grow up quickly these days."

"I've got an older, better-looking brother; our house was always full of girls. I hated the bastard until some of his cast-offs started giving me the eye." Alistair smiled at her. "I couldn't believe my luck."

"Well, if you're anything to go by, I'd sure like to meet your brother." Carly chuckled and crossed her legs.

Alistair was suddenly taken aback with the possibility that he might just have received a compliment.

"Denbigh! Not too far out! I don't care if you can swim the English Channel! Stay this side of the buoys!" Alistair's head swivelled from left to right before turning to smile at Carly standing next to him on the shoreline. "Do you like my lighthouse impression? I thought watching my own three on the beach was stressful enough; now I've got fourteen of the buggers."

"You watch Denbigh, and I'll look after the rest." Carly's laugh tinkled along with the foaming waves. "The rest of them seem quite easy anyway; they just want to paddle and muck about, although Adrienne seems quite intent on staying as near to you as she can."

"Yes, I had noticed but I'm trying to ignore it." Alistair whispered with a smile. "Thank God they're all not like those two. Imagine them all swimming off in different directions; what a nightmare." Alistair watched Jack Denbigh's confident, even strokes as he cut through the water.

"How old are your children?" Carly dipped one toe in the sea hesitantly.

"Tom's seventeen now, and Jake's as old as this lot. Jessie's thirteen. They're not bad kids; they've even almost stopped fighting now, which makes life a bit easier. Have you got any?" He looked down at her toenails, which were painted bright red.

"Nah; not yet. Never found a bloke willing to stay around long enough to give me any." She laughed ruefully and retreated back onto the sand. "I was never that maternal anyway."

"Plenty of time yet; you don't look a day over twenty five to me." He took off an extra five years just to make sure of an agreeable response.

"Hah! I'm thirty four actually, but I'll pass on the kids, thanks. Too much of a tie, and I can't function without any sleep."

"Yeah, I remember that, although Ann did the lion's share at the time." He scuffed some sand with his foot and tried not to focus on her mesmerising wind-whipped curls.

"Who's out there with Denbigh?" Carly strained her eyes seawards.

"Shit. It's Sanderson; probably trying to impress his girlfriend." Alistair whipped off his t-shirt and sandals. "Back in a mo."

Even in mid-summer the English Channel was cold. Alistair winced as the waves soaked his nether regions, and ignoring several wolf-whistles from the girls, swam steadily out until he was in earshot of Denbigh and Sanderson:

"You two! You're too far out! Get back towards the shore…now!" He indicated with a thumb for extra effect whilst treading water.

"Oh, but Sir……!" Jack Denbigh grabbed hold of Kevin Sanderson's head and pushed him under the waves.

"Denbigh, if you and Sanderson don't get back now, then you'll both be grounded on the sand for the rest of the day."

"Okay, okay; we're going."

Muttering to each other, the two boys swam back. Alistair, dripping and shivering, followed them out of the water and then flopped down on the sand.

"I'm well impressed with your life-saving skills." Carly laughed. "Nice hairy chest too."

"It's a rug." Alistair joked. "It's stuck on."

CHAPTER 6

THE HOTEL BAR was virtually empty. Alistair, pint of beer in hand, perched on a stool and wondered if Carly would keep her promise. The delicious vision in his head of them sitting together with no interruptions for one or two stolen hours kept him constantly looking towards the stairs and tapping one foot impatiently on the bar stool. After downing two pints in half an hour, he was just about to give it up as a bad job when out of the corner of his eye he was aware of movement on the stairwell. Turning around his heart started to beat faster at the sight of her, red curls shining in the spotlights, and womanly curves half hidden by an ivory sleeveless mini-dress.

"Ah, you remembered then!" He bent further towards the bar to cover his growing erection.

"Yeah; the girls took ages to go to sleep, but it's all quiet on the Western front at the moment." Carly chuckled. "They certainly like to chatter though."

"The boys were out like a light. I imagined toothpaste fights, Denbigh whacking everyone with pillows, and Sanderson bog-brushing Pritchard, but I think the afternoon on the beach must have worn them out." He was aware of gabbling like a madman to try and cover his nervousness. "Can I get you a drink?"

"Yes please; a bottle of cold cider sounds very good right at this moment."

As she sat cool and collected on the adjacent stool, he tried very hard not to notice that her dress had ridden up to expose more of her bare thighs. Mentally cursing his stiffened penis, he waved to the barman.

"These stools are uncomfortable. Shall we sit over there?" Carly indicated towards two unoccupied armchairs in a corner of the bar.

"Er… yeah. You go over and I'll be there in a minute." He hoped his summer shirt flowing casually outside a clean pair of khaki shorts would conceal the tell-tale bulge.

Thankfully she had picked the chair facing away from him. Alistair carried the drinks over to where she sat cross-legged and radiant, noticing how her fiery mane attracted attention not only from the barman, but every now and then was also receiving covert stares from the male half of two middle-aged couples in the bar.

"Cheers, Ali. You're a life-saver…..literally!" She grinned as she poured some cider.

"They weren't in any trouble; just arsing about." He took a swig of beer and feasted his eyes upon her.

"Would you have let your own kids swim out that far?" Her pale blue eyes met his as she raised her glass to her lips.

"The older one, yes. The younger two, no." Alistair felt hot under the collar, and bowled over by her beauty. "I was just making sure my name wasn't on tomorrow's headlines."

"Yeah. I can just see it." Carly laughed. "'Teacher sunbathes on beach while children drown'."

"Plural; teach*ers* don't forget." Alistair waggled a finger at her.

"We'd be forever vilified, even though I can't swim."

"You can't swim?" He looked at her in surprise.

"Confession time. No, I never learned how, and to be honest, I never regretted it until today." She exhaled slowly and poured more cider into her glass.

"They'll be busy anyway for the rest of the week; hopefully we won't have a repeat performance." He leaned back in his chair and smiled. "Didn't your parents ever take you swimming? Sorry to be nosey, I'm just curious."

"That's okay. Dad was conspicuously absent for most of my childhood, and Mum was too busy working and looking after me and my sister and brother to ever bother about going swimming. My brother can swim like a fish and my sister learned eventually, but I never did." Carly shrugged.

He tried to imagine another stunning redhead with blue eyes sitting before him.

"Are you the eldest?" He began to feel more relaxed as he finished a third pint of beer.

"No, the youngest; the baby of the family, so I wasn't expected to do anything other than to enjoy being pampered. My sister eventually married an American and lives out in Detroit, but my brother's close by; he's nearly forty now. I see my sister for a couple of weeks once a year during the summer holidays." She took another sip of her drink and put her glass down on a side table, re-crossing her legs.

"And *were* you pampered? I'm forty two; an absolute Methuselah unfortunately." Alistair kept his eyes above her shoulders. "I've even got to wear reading glasses now."

"You look younger than my brother." She smiled as her eyes met his. "Was I pampered? Ha, I was wrapped in cotton wool from birth; it's a wonder I ever learned to walk!"

"Ann often accuses me of mollycoddling Jessie, our thirteen year old. I don't know; with the boys I can have a rough and tumble, but Jessie's my princess I suppose." He smiled with the memory of his daughter's warm arms around his neck.

"You sound a lovely father; your kids are lucky." Carly grimaced. "I never really knew my dad at all."

"Did he die then, or what?" Alistair looked at her with interest.

"No, he's still alive…somewhere, living with his third or fourth wife; I lost count." She picked up her glass again and drained it. "He put Mum through hell; what a bastard." Her eyes narrowed as she sighed.

"Sorry to hear that. I hope he hasn't put you off men for life." Alistair gave a wry laugh. "We're not all womanisers, you know. Some of us have been married for years; like me." He rolled his eyes. "It's my thousandth anniversary in September."

"Wow! You're looking good on it!" She gave a hoot of laughter. "Well done you."

"Another drink?" Alistair struggled for something to fill the sudden vacuum.

"Just one more cider, and then I'll call it a night." Carly nodded. "The last thing I want tomorrow when I'm walking around Osborne House is a hangover."

He inspected her delightful rear view undetected as he walked back from the bar. Her hair, so much thicker and curlier than Ann's, cascaded down to her shoulders in waves and ringlets, making him want to reach out and run his fingers through it. Her arms, lightly tanned and freckled, lay still and relaxed on the armrests.

"One glass of cider for the lady." His voice sounded thicker as he took one last glimpse of her thighs. "Here's to a great week." He raised a shot of whisky.

"Cheers." She smiled and took a swig. "Some of the staff at St Luke's I've found to be a bit on the stuffy side, but you seem quite normal."

"Until it gets to midnight and then I turn into a werewolf." Alistair yawned.

"Oh yes, the hairy chest; I'd forgotten about that. Am I keeping you up?" Her mirth rose along with the bubbles in her glass.

"Not in the least. I'm ready to hit the town in a minute. Is there a nightclub in Shanklin?" He called her bluff, pleasantly relaxed.

"You seem to have forgotten; we've got fourteen children to look after." Carly snorted with laughter.

"And you don't look a day over twenty. I don't know how you do it."

Alistair suddenly giggled, aware that their conversation was being overheard by at least one, if not both, of the middle-aged couples.

"Talk about being chained to the sink, barefoot and pregnant. You really need to get the snip now. Fourteen is more than enough." Carly took another swig of cider. "You're worse than a bloody stud bull."

"I've only got to sneeze and whoop-de-do, there's another one!" His giggling was getting hard to control. "You'll have to go back on the streets; I don't seem to be earning enough money anymore."

"Come on tiger; bedtime." Carly finished her drink and winked at the couple to her left. "But we'd better check on the kids first."

They were still grinning as they walked out of the bar and up the stairs. Alistair, disappointed that the evening had come to an end, touched Carly's arm briefly as he carried on up to the second floor.

"Thanks for the laugh; see you tomorrow."

"Yeah; I'll be ready. Night night, tiger." She gave him a brief wave and then was gone.

CHAPTER 7

"SIR, I DON'T like eating a full English breakfast first thing in the morning." Adrienne Draper wrinkled her nose in disgust. "It'll make me sick."

"It's gross." Keira Trelawny stepped out of the breakfast buffet queue in horror. "I'm a vegetarian."

"The alternatives are cornflakes or something like toast and jam." Alistair, plate in hand, moved along and speared a sausage, waving to Carly as she came in the door. "Tucker; try and make sure there's something left for everyone else."

"Sorry Sir, I'm starving." Leon Tucker, plate piled high with cholesterol, helped himself to another fried egg.

"Everybody's here now." Carly finished counting the heads and then joined the end of the queue. "Adrienne and Keira, just take some cereal and toast and have something more at lunchtime, or I could ask them to do you some porridge if you like."

"Ugh. I hate porridge." Keira grimaced. "I'll have a few cornflakes."

"I'll have toast." Adrienne walked over to the toaster and

grabbed some bread. "Shall I get you some, Sir?"

"No, just do your own, thanks. The tables reserved for us are the four over by the window."

Alistair was beginning to find Adrienne's constant presence slightly irritating; the girl had stuck to him like glue for most of the afternoon on the beach, and now seemed to be following him everywhere. Whilst helping himself to baked beans and supervising the remaining stragglers, he could see out of the corner of his eye that although her toast was ready she was holding out on finding a seat. He sighed and caught Carly's eye as she moved nearer to him in the queue.

"Adrienne, please go and sit down now." Carly ladled some mushrooms and tomatoes onto three sausages. "Your toast will be cold otherwise."

"Cheers for that." Alistair whispered under his breath. "I think I've got myself a stalker."

"No problem." Carly grinned.

"How far is it to Osborne House, Sir?"

Alistair looked in the rear view mirror and could see that Adrienne had wormed herself into the seat behind him.

"Roughly half an hour. It's only about 60 miles all the way around the coastline, so it doesn't take very long to get anywhere."

"Good," replied Adrienne. "Otherwise Celie will be sick again."

"Celie, let me know if you feel ill." Carly looked over her shoulder at Celie, sitting next to Adrienne.

"I'm okay. I forgot to take my travel pill yesterday." Celie smiled and turned on her iPod.

"Right, seat belts on; the ones at the back, that means you!"

Alistair checked in the mirror that Denbigh and Sanderson were complying, and then started up the engine and pulled out of the hotel car park. He felt more relaxed with Carly following their pleasant interlude the night before, and looked forward to a possible replay later that evening. As far as he could tell, Carly's manner seemed more laid-back and natural too, and he returned her smile as she sat pretty and good enough to eat to the left of him in the front passenger seat.

"Who knows what the ancient Romans used to call the Isle of Wight?" He chuckled as he joined the morning traffic jam along the High Street. "There's a prize for the first one to tell me the correct answer. For your clue the answer lies in this queue of traffic in front of us."

"Civic". Gillian Lister's voice piped up.

"No, try again."

"Is it Rover, Sir?" Adrienne Draper craned her neck past him to see out of the front window.

"Nope."

"Rav." Robert Evans' voice boomed from somewhere near the back.

"Behave yourself, Evans." Alistair smiled and moved up to second gear.

"I know, Sir, it's Vectis." Kylie Morris giggled. "It's on the bus there."

"Sir! She just Googled it on her phone!" Freddie Peterson's indignant voice carried over to the front. "I saw her!"

"No prizes for cheating, Kylie." Alistair put on a serious voice. "I'm keeping it fair."

"Oh, sorry." Kylie blushed and her features took on a sheepish look.

"Here's another one." Carly turned around. "Who is the Isle of Wight's most famous prisoner? The one who gets it right can pick out a small prize in Osborne's gift shop, and I do *not* want to see any phones. I'm keeping watch for cheaters."

"Ronnie Biggs." Leon Tucker raised his hand.

"No, Tucker; nice try though."

"Ronnie Kray?" Oliver Stewart suggested hopefully.

"No, sorry Oliver. Have another go." Carly smiled.

"We want a clue, Miss." Gillian Lister looked blank.

"We'll be visiting the actual room in Carisbrooke Castle where he was imprisoned tomorrow. He tried to escape, but got stuck between the bars on the window."

"I know! I know!" Keira Trelawny forgetting her erstwhile cool, composed exterior, bounced up and down on her seat. "It's Charles the first! Mr Carter told us about that in History last year!"

"Well done, Keira. You can pick out something small from the gift shop after we've looked around the house and grounds today." Carly gave Keira a thumbs up and turned around to face the front again.

"Can we have another question, Sir? We all want a prize." Tyler Marshall turned sideways and gave Keira the evil eye.

"Okay, here's the last one, because if I give you all a prize I'll have no money left. Also it'll get busy at Newport and I'll have to concentrate."

"What's the question, Sir?" Adrienne Draper moved nearer to Celie so that she could see herself in the rear view mirror.

"Who owns Osborne House?" Alistair winked at Carly, who smiled.

"Queen Victoria!" Kevin Sanderson shouted from the back.

"She's dead, dickhead." Jack Denbigh laughed and gave him a kick.

"The Queen?" Adrienne craned her neck to see into the rear view mirror.

"Not the Queen exactly." Alistair shook his head and kept his eyes on the road. "Keep trying."

"Elton John?" Kylie Morris ventured timidly.

"Elton John?" Carly mouthed to Alistair and muffled a snort. "Er…no, Kylie, I'm afraid not."

"David Beckham!" Kevin Sanderson shouted from the back.

Alistair tried hard to keep a straight face as he negotiated the bus around Newport's Coppins' Bridge roundabout.

"I'll tell you; it's us….the nation, well English Heritage actually. Edward the seventh gave it to the nation after Queen Victoria's death. But you'll all be interested to see Seaclose Park in a minute. Who knows what happens at Seaclose Park every second weekend of June?"

"I know! I know, Sir!" Lisa Lambert waved a hand in the air. "My mum and dad took me there last year! The Isle of Wight Festival! Yeah! I saw Jon Bon Jovi!"

"He's old." Leon Tucker, nonplussed, sucked on a gobstopper.

"That's right, Lisa. We'll see the park coming up on our left soon." Alistair, relieved to be in the right lane, followed the signs to East Cowes.

"Can I get something from the gift shop then please?" Lisa wheedled.

"Okay; something small, and I *mean* something small." Alistair indicated with his left arm. "Over there; that's where the stage was."

"How do you know all this, Sir?" Adrienne followed the others and looked to the left.

"Because I grew up here." He noticed Carly's quick look of interest. "I moved to the mainland when I left home."

CHAPTER 8

OSBORNE'S CAR PARK was already filling up by the time they arrived. Alistair brought the bus to a halt in a shady corner, and turned off the engine. He stretched, yawned, and then opened the doors:

"All out! Stay together. I need to get a group ticket first."

He was aware that Carly had come to stand beside him as they waited for the last ones to climb out of the bus:

"I never knew you used to live here." She hoisted her bag onto her shoulder and looked at him quizzically.

"It was a long time ago. My parents lived in Ventnor. I was eighteen and wanted to see a bit of life and so went to university in London." Alistair locked the bus and pocketed the keys.

"Do they still live there?" Carly walked along beside him at the back of the group. "You were so lucky to be brought up here."

"Mum and Dad are both dead now, but the house was passed to my brother and me. We do stay in it quite a lot; it's nice to have all the family together sometimes." He smiled whilst signalling to the group. "Wait here with Miss Jessop everyone! I'm going in to get a ticket."

"Wow, I'd love to have lived in Queen Victoria's age!" Alistair, noticing how Adrienne never seemed to be more than two feet away from him at any one time, chuckled on seeing her gazing around the room with awe at the acid-yellow silk curtains and sofas resplendent in the drawing room.

"This was how the rich people lived; it was somewhat different for the poor. Trust me, you wouldn't have liked it at all." He smiled as he gently teased her. "You would have had to exist without iPhones, iPods, iPads, Kindles, and the Internet."

"I could do that. I would have read or played my CD's"

"I want to have a go on that pool table over there." Jack pointed towards the end of the L-shaped room.

"It's a billiard table actually, and it's down one end like that so the men could play after dinner out of sight of the Queen." Alistair kept a straight face whilst imagining Queen Victoria investigating the intricacies of a CD player, and David Beckham kicking a ball about with the little princes on the lawn.

"Didn't she like billiards then?" Adrienne chewed some gum absent-mindedly.

"Yes, she played in the afternoons. But the men did manly things like smoking, drinking brandy and playing billiards after dinner, and the ladies sat around chatting, sewing, or playing musical instruments." He pointed to a well-preserved harp.

"Sounds boring." Lisa sighed. "I'd rather play billiards with the men."

"Apart from the Queen, women had to know their place." Carly piped up. "There were no equal opportunities back then."

"That sucks." Adrienne shook her head.

"Blokes are in charge, so get used to it." Kevin looked down on Adrienne from his lofty height of nearly six feet.

"Drop dead Kevin." Adrienne waved him away with one hand.

"Don't tell him to drop dead." Lisa gave Adrienne a glare.

"Let's move swiftly on. We can go upstairs and look at the bedrooms and nursery." Carly ushered the group out of the room. "Who knows how many children the Queen and Prince Albert had?"

"Twelve?" Leon sucked on a fresh gobstopper.

"Not quite." Carly laughed. "Any more guesses?"

"Is there a prize?" Gillian enquired hopefully.

"No, not this time. This is just to improve your general knowledge." Carly looked around the group. "Give up?"

"Ten?" Celie ventured.

"Nearly; she had nine. In the grounds is the Swiss Chalet with a tiny kitchen, where Prince Albert taught them to grow their own vegetables and cook. We can walk down there soon."

"Nine kids! Didn't they have a TV?" Robert grinned.

"Not in the eighteen fifties, Robert." Carly shook her head and smiled.

"Perhaps somebody should have invented one Miss, then they might have only had two."

"Oh, just look at all those little cots lined up!" Celie Ingram squealed with delight.

"Ugh; there's babies' legs and arms on the table!" Gillian wrinkled her nose.

Alistair suddenly wished he could have kept a souvenir cast of one of Jessie's tiny baby arms. He remembered the exquisite pudginess of it, making him want to virtually eat the limb without even spitting out the bones.

"Victorians often had plaster casts made of their children's limbs for safekeeping. The Queen was no exception."

"It's gross!" Keira shuddered.

"It's only plaster. It's not like it's a real arm that's been preserved." Michael shrugged.

"It's still gross." Keira turned away.

Alistair caught up with Carly as the group moved towards Queen Victoria's bedroom:

"Any sign of Elton John?"

"Perhaps he's in the old girl's bed next door." Carly whispered. "Where do these kids get their ideas from?"

"Did she die on this actual bed Sir?" Adrienne gazed at the ornate double bed with its bronze memorial plaque.

"It's probably a replica, I'd say." Alistair shook his head. "But much of the other furniture is original."

"It's a bit eerie in here, isn't it?" Carly whispered in Alistair's ear. "You can imagine the fire crackling in the grate, the clock ticking away the minutes, and all the family standing around the bed waiting for her to die."

"Yeah, sometimes I'd love to be clairvoyant and go back to nineteen-o-one and just be part of it." Alistair nodded. "You think like me, don't you? Ann always prefers to get out of this room as quickly as possible, but something makes me want to push all the visitors out of the door so I can sit and soak up the atmosphere in peace."

"You're right. I could stay in here all day." Carly sighed.

"Where did she go to the loo?" Kevin broke unwelcoming into Alistair's reverie.

"There's a shower and toilet next door. Very modern for the times. There's even an old wind-up lift that was installed when she was too old and lame to walk up the stairs." Alistair smiled. "So you see, Sanderson, she wasn't too badly off despite an obvious lack of Wi-Fi."

"Wow! This is cool! Look at the swords, Kev!" Jack Denbigh surveyed the Durbar room with awe.

"Queen Victoria was crowned Empress of India in 1897. She never actually went to India, but in this room are stored all the gifts she was given by individuals and communities from that country to celebrate the event. There are also paintings of her Indian servants which she had commissioned." Alistair was pleased to see the two boys enjoying a little piece of history.

"You love this place, don't you?" Carly looked at him and smiled.

"Does it show? My parents first brought me here when I was about seven. I think I know this house better than the old Queen herself." Alistair chuckled.

"You bring it alive for them. I can see they're getting something out of it." Carly nodded.

"Hopefully they'll remember it all their lives like I did." He gave her arm a nudge with his elbow. "Although it would have been nice if Sir Elton could have been home today to play the harpsichord."

CHAPTER 9

"HAVE WE GOT to walk a whole mile, Sir?" Keira tossed her long red hair and sighed.

"You can get that courtesy bus over there down to the Swiss Cottage, but it'll be full of *old* people." Alistair frowned. "They'll all be over forty at least."

"I'll walk."

Keira ran to join the rest of the group, leaving Alistair and Carly to amble along together at the back:

"Cheers; I'll be old in six years then." Carly poked her tongue out at him.

"Well, I'm forty two; what does that make me?" He laughed.

"Bloody ancient."

"I shouldn't be out really. I need to be sitting on a pot somewhere with a rug around me."

"Sitting on a pot?" Carly laughed. "Surely it's better to be sitting on a rug with pot around you?"

"Ah, now you're talking! Have you got a joint? Adrienne's beginning to get on my mammaries." Alistair began to enjoy the banter.

"I thought it best not to bring any on a school trip, but I've got a nice little stash at home." Carly grinned. "My brother's mate has a cannabis farm in his loft."

"Good God!" Alistair roared with laughter. "I haven't smoked any pot since leaving university!"

"Shh! The kids will hear! I often find it quite relaxing actually." Carly lowered her voice and pushed some hair back from her face. "I'll give you some to try when we get home."

"I can just imagine Ann's face when she sees me comfortably numb and smoking a spliff!" Alistair giggled.

"Your kids will think you're really cool though." Carly grinned.

"They'll think I've flipped my lid." He suddenly had a vision of himself and Carly sprawled naked on a rug, sharing a post-coital spliff in front of a roaring fire.

"Give me a lift home on Friday before you take the bus back, and I'll give you some."

"Bugger off." Alistair chuckled, tearing himself away from the mental image. "I'll give you a lift home, but you can keep hold of your stash."

"As you prefer." Carly's eyes twinkled. "Although you might need some after a week with this lot."

"Oh, this is really cute!" Kylie surveyed the Swiss Cottage with admiration.

"If you look at the surrounding gardens, each child had their own allotment marked out where they grew vegetables." Alistair indicated towards nine miniature wheelbarrows and half size gardening tools. "They cooked whatever they grew in the little kitchen inside; come and take a look."

One by one they filtered into the cottage, with Alistair and Carly bringing up the rear:

"Everything's tiny, Sir!" Adrienne, two steps away from Alistair, looked up at him in wonder.

"If you go upstairs, you'll see the sitting room where the children served meals to their parents." Alistair noticed how the girls seemed more interested than the boys.

"I've had to do this for real for a long time, not mucking about in a doll's house." Lisa shrugged.

"Oh" Carly gently coaxed. "Why's that?"

"Mum works. I always cook dinner for Mum, me and my little sister."

"Good for you." Carly refrained from enquiring any further.

"When's lunchtime?" Leon yawned.

"Now, if you like. There's a picnic area outside where we can eat our packed lunches. Those who've seen enough of the cottage can come with me, and those who want to see upstairs need to stay with Miss Jessop."

Alistair made his way outside to a shady patch of grass, amused to find all eight boys following behind him like overgrown ducklings. By the time he noticed Carly's legs coming down the steps of the cottage, he could see that the boys had more or less finished eating.

"What can we do now, Sir?" Kevin zipped up his rucksack, ready to go."

"There's a museum over there." Alistair pointed to his right. "You'll be able to see all the children's collections over the years; for instance there's fossils, butterflies, and stuffed animals and birds in there, and also their toys. Go and have a look while the girls eat their lunch. If you don't fancy that, there's the Queen's private beach over to my left and what remains of her bathing machine."

"Okay, we'll have a butcher's then." Kevin stood up with Jack and Tyler.

"Be back here in an hour." Alistair looked at his watch. "I'm going to stay here and eat my lunch."

"Thank God, they've all wandered off!" Carly yawned. "I've got post-lunch dip now. I could lay down here and go straight to sleep."

"Me too; shame they're all coming back in about ten minutes." Alistair feasted his eyes on Carly's burnished locks, fiery under the early afternoon sun. "Fancy a spliff?"

"Don't start that again!" She hugged her knees, laughing.

"Isn't your brother's mate worried that he'll get found out?" Alistair asked seriously.

"He's been doing it for years. He's careful not to grow too much. He doesn't sell it; it's just for friends and family." Carly nodded. "There's usually trouble when you start dealing I think."

"I wouldn't know; I'm a respectable member of society." He laughed.

"Oh, yeah, as innocent as the day's long." She rolled her eyes. "Come on then Mister Whiter than White, what did you get up to in your mis-spent youth?"

"Have you got the voice recorder running?" He glanced towards her bag.

"Yeah, I'm going to reveal all on YouTube as soon as your back's turned." She kept a hint of a smile on her face.

"Me and a mate broke into Shanklin Chine one night and scared each other shitless jumping out from behind the ferns in the dark." He grinned. "I got absolutely wrecked at the Rock Island festival in 2002. I wanted to see Robert Plant sing, but spent the evening in the First Aid tent throwing up. Ann wouldn't speak to me for a week." He grinned.

"Yeah, we've all done that." She lowered her voice. "For your information I once had a rather pleasant communal orgasm in a tent at Glastonbury."

"A *communal* orgasm?" He tried to keep the desperate interest out of his voice.

"Yeah; first and last time though. No protection; nothing. I shudder to think what I might have caught. It's amazing the things you do when you're young and silly, isn't it?"

With the return of Denbigh and Sanderson infiltrating Alistair's joyful daydream of campfire climaxes, the intimate moment collapsed just as surely as if the boys had pulled up the tent pegs themselves.

CHAPTER 10

"I THINK THE kids got something out of today." Carly raised her glass. "Cheers. Sir did a grand job."

"Miss wasn't exactly resting on her laurels either." Alistair clinked his glass with Carly's, noticing with approval her low-cut pale lemon sundress. "Thanks for everything." *Especially for the communal orgasm story.*

"No probs. What's next on the agenda?"

"Carisbrooke Castle; we'll just have to ensure that Denbigh doesn't tip Pritchard over the ramparts." Alistair took a swig of beer. "Anyway, cheers! Here's to even more fun at Carisbrooke than in your tent at Glastonbury." He grinned and touched her glass again with his own.

"Oh, God, don't start that again." She grimaced. "It wasn't my tent. I can't even remember whose tent it was or how we ended up in there. I worried for weeks afterwards in case I'd caught a dose or even worse, got pregnant."

"I don't know where you went to university, but there was always a long line of despondent looking students waiting patiently to be seen at our medical centre on a Monday morning." Alistair chuckled. "Don't worry; even I once had to have the shameful antibiotic jab in the arse 'just to be on the safe side."

"Only the one time though, I'll bet." She waggled her forefinger at him. "What with you being so respectable and all."

"I sometimes miss those days." He sighed. "But I suppose the real reason is that I'm missing my golden, carefree youth; no worries about keeping up with the mortgage payments back then."

"So, would you do things any differently if you could go back to being twenty again?" She fixed two candid blue eyes on him.

"I wouldn't have lost the love of my life." Alistair wondered why he was suddenly telling a virtual stranger something that even Ann did not know.

"Oh? Come on then; out with it. You've got me interested now." Carly laid down her glass, put her elbows on the table, and rested her chin on both hands.

"Maggie was my first love. She and I were inseparable at university for that first year, but stupid me went and bolloxed it up."

With a sting of pain he remembered that drunken evening as though it were yesterday; Leila laying on top of him, and the look on Maggie's face as she came in the room.

"Hence the antibiotics in the arse?" Carly asked hopefully.

"Yeah, something like that." He suddenly felt like crying.

"But hey, you didn't hang around long; you found someone who wanted your babies. I've been looking for that person for years, but I think he buggered off as soon as he saw me coming." She shrugged.

"One more drink? This is getting maudlin." He downed the rest of his pint in one go and stood up.

"Sure; make it another G and T."

As he stood at the bar he looked over at the back of Carly's head and knew without a shadow of a doubt that the woman he was having a quick end-of-day drink with was making him feel a little too relaxed; in fact more agreeable and laid-back than he had felt in a long time. When carrying the drinks back to their table he let his gaze linger on the slope of her shoulders and the thin straps of her sundress. His penis began a somersault in his trousers:

"One G and T for the lady."

"Ta. They're not bad kids really, are they?" She smiled at him as she took the glass.

"All you need to do is get them interested, and then you've got them." He nodded and sat back down. "Plus adding in a few laughs here and there as well; that's always a good one."

"Did you always want to go into teaching?" Carly sipped her drink and looked at him enquiringly.

"Absolutely. I know it sounds corny, but I get so much out of it." He sighed.

"I can see that. In fact anyone with half an ounce of sense can see it." She smiled.

"How about you?" He looked at her. "Have you found your niche in life?"

"God knows." She laughed. "I lurch from one hare-brained scheme to the next, although this one seems to be lasting the distance."

"Keep at it. The kids love you." He ached to touch her. "Denbigh especially."

"Only because he loves looking down my cleavage." She hooted with laughter. "His eyes were nearly popping out of his head this afternoon."

"I can't blame him there. What is it they say? Weapons of mass distraction?" Alistair sat back in his seat and crossed his legs.

"Sexist pig." She grinned and folded her arms across her bosom.

"I'm only a bloke." He shrugged. "Us men are just life support systems for our penises; at least that's what Ann always tells me."

"Ann seems like a sensible lady."

"Yeah, she is." He said, suddenly coming back to reality.

"But you'd like it if ……. sometimes she wasn't so sensible?"

Alistair gazed into Carly's laughing eyes and had a sudden inkling of what could happen if he let it. Ann was two hundred miles away, and a possible chance to taste the luscious but forbidden peach in front of him might probably never come his way again:

"She will always be sensible." The blood rose to his face. "But at times like this….. hell, sometimes you just have to throw sensible and respectable to the wind don't you?"

The silence between them was electric, charged with a myriad of thoughts unsaid. When he felt her fingers lightly stroking his forearm he tried to control his breathing, which to his disgust had started to come in quick, noisy rasps:

"I've got one sachet of coffee left in my room. You're welcome to it, but you'll have to come in and get it." Carly's fingertips caressed his own.

"Any sugar?" Alistair, lost in the blue of her eyes, placed one hand over hers.

"Heaps of the stuff; as much as you like, tiger."

He knew it was madness, but the thrill of the chase had blinded him to the consequences of his actions. He rose to his feet and followed her to the first floor; his heart hammering a fevered rhythm in his chest as he feasted his eyes on two tanned and freckled legs ascending the stairs.

The corridor was quiet; no sound could be heard coming from the girls' three twin rooms. He closed his eyes and stood close behind her while she quietly opened the door to the bedroom. Her perfume was overpowering; he was lost in her voice, her hair, the very essence of her. He tried to remember in that split second if he had ever felt this way before about his wife. He knew that Ann was solid and dependable, and could be relied on to protect the children and to always do the right thing. However, as he walked behind Carly into the bedroom, he realised his wife lacked the kind of free spirit that Carly possessed; the element of danger that was like an aphrodisiac to him. He had never found this before in any woman apart from Leila. He could not resist it at university, and he could not resist it now.

She switched on the bedside lamp, and came to stand smiling before him; youthful beauty not yet marred by sagging middle age. Slowly he lowered the straps of her sundress and she stepped out of it. With growing excitement he saw she was naked underneath except for a brief pair of lacy panties, the kind he had bought for Ann once but she had put away in a drawer and never worn.

"God; you're beautiful." He exhaled slowly, taking in every inch of her.

"Have you ever had a woman undress you before?" Carly kissed him, her tongue probing his mouth greedily, as she began to unbutton his shirt.

"My mum used to." He laughed and put his arms around her, sliding her panties down with one easy movement of his hands.

"Enjoy it."

She stepped out of her underwear and slid down his chest onto her knees. He ran his hands over the top of her head, fingering her soft red curls in wonder as she unzipped his jeans and caressed his erection through the thin cotton of his boxers, unhurriedly moving his clothing down onto the floor. He kept one hand on her hair, closed his eyes, and relished the sensation of her tongue as it licked the shaft of his penis and moved slowly upwards towards the tip. By the time she had expertly applied a condom, his whole being was screaming for release. Moving back and stepping out of his lower garments, he put his hands underneath her armpits, lifted her up and carried her over to the bed, where she lay smiling underneath him like a modern-day Scheherazade, the tip of her tongue tantalisingly flicking out to lick her lips. Kneeling over her he moved his hands across her full breasts, gently kneading the nipples while she moaned slightly and arched her back.

Alistair was enveloped in a tidal wave of emotion as Carly parted her knees. Moving on top of her, he passed the point of no return as she guided him skilfully into her velvet core. He quickly found her rhythm, moving against her in perfect harmony; creating a symphony of exquisite sensations that he knew would remain in his memory forever.

CHAPTER 11

HE CURSED AS the razor slipped and a trickle of blood appeared above his upper lip. Alistair tore off a piece of toilet paper and dabbed the small gash, knowing with dismay that it would probably now remain bleeding throughout breakfast. Out in the corridor he could hear Sanderson teasing Pritchard again. He sighed, feeling wracked with guilt, yet strangely uplifted on bringing to mind the vision of Carly's milky body in the lamplight. He knew what happened between them would have to be a one-off; he was Head of the English department for God's sake! The position called for respectability, morality, decorum, and loyalty to one's wife and family, not wanton fornication with any new, young member of staff at the least opportunity.

Pocketing his room key, he straightened his shirt, put on his trainers, checked his flies were zipped, and opened the door to his room.

"'Morning Sanderson. 'Morning Pritchard. Everybody ready?"

"Yeah. You're bleeding, Sir." Kevin pointed to his upper lip.

"I know; believe me, I know."

"You've cut yourself shaving, Sir." Jack Denbigh grinned as he followed Leon out of the bedroom.

"Put a sock in it, Denbigh." Alistair rolled his eyes. "Come on, let's get at that cooked breakfast."

As they passed by the first floor he could hear Carly's voice in one of the rooms chivvying the girls along. He decided he would not say anything to her at breakfast at all, in case one of the teenagers picked up on a look, a knowing smile, or some secret nod. He queued up at the buffet, took a plate of sausages, beans, fried egg and mushrooms, and sat down facing a window with his back to the door. When he heard her come in with the girls he spread jam on a slice of toast and chewed thoughtfully.

"'Morning boys! 'Morning Mr Veale!" Carly's voice was bright and breezy.

"Morning Miss." Eight boys stopped chewing momentarily to chant in unison."

"Hi." Alistair felt himself reddening as he turned halfway around. "Ready for Carisbrooke Castle today?"

"Absolutely. I could eat a horse though; can't think why I'm so hungry." Carly shot him a quick, meaningful glance before taking her place in the buffet queue.

"Is there a café at the castle, Sir?" Leon took Oliver Stewart's unwanted slice of toast and bit into it.

"Yes, don't worry Tucker. You won't go hungry." Alistair was grateful to the boy for changing the subject. "Boys and girls; as soon as you've all finished eating and are ready to go, wait for me in the foyer." He put down his knife and fork and stood up, suddenly wanting to be away from Carly's mesmerising presence and to be able to gather his thoughts together. Ignoring her look of surprise he stood up, walked out of the dining room, and took the stairs two at a time back up to the second floor.

"Everything alright, tiger? You've been a bit quiet on the way here." She hung back with him as the group climbed out of the minibus and started walking towards the castle entrance.

"Just a bit embarrassed today; sorry." He shook his head. "Last night should never have happened."

"But it did. I enjoyed it; didn't you?" She shrugged. "I hope you're not going to go all sanctimonious and whiter-than-white on me?"

"Look; I've been married for nigh on twenty years. I have the most loyal, steadfast wife any man could ever want." He sighed. "Let me feel a little bit of guilt, please."

"But only for a minute or two; just before you go off to hell in a handcart." Carly snorted with laughter. "Come on, lighten up. We had a quick fuck; what's wrong with that?"

"Only that I've broken my marriage vows." Alistair sighed. "I'm not in the habit of sleeping around, you know."

"We didn't do much sleeping, tiger." She grinned. "In fact, I'm knackered this morning!"

"Me too. I couldn't sleep all night; now I've got to walk round the bloody castle all day with this lot." He sighed.

"That'll teach you to keep it in your pocket then." She tossed her head and stepped up her pace; catching up with the rest of the group and leaving Alistair trailing behind miserably.

"Look at that house down there in the middle of the courtyard, Sir!" Adrienne, trekking along the castle ramparts next to Alistair at the head of the group, pointed a finger over the edge and looked up at him.

"Princess Beatrice, Queen Victoria's youngest child, used it as a summer house until her death in 1944." Alistair ignored the sandpaper in his eyes and raised his voice to project to the back of the group. "On the way back we can stop nearby at St Mildred's church, Whippingham, if you like, and see the tomb where she is buried alongside her husband."

"Oh yes please, Sir." Adrienne nodded.

"Have we got to?" Jack questioned. "I'd rather stay here and look round the castle."

"We'll see enough of the castle today, don't worry." Alistair yawned. "In half an hour is a demonstration of how water was drawn from the well using a donkey wheel in the days gone by, and then there's a guided tour of the castle after lunch."

"What's a donkey wheel?" Kevin asked.

"Well, the poor old donkey walked round and round on a wheel in the well-house. The wheel turned, and surprise, surprise, up came a bucket of water from the depths." Alistair grinned. "Who wants to see it working?"

"That's cruel!" Kylie shook her head.

"Yeah! Donkey power!" Kevin shouted.

"Donkeys stink." Keira gave a thumbs down.

"All those in favour?" Alistair looked at the number of raised hands.

"I'll take those in who want to have a look." Carly nodded. "The rest of you can hang around outside in the courtyard with Mr Veale."

"I want some lunch." Leon Tucker announced.

"We'll finish walking the ramparts, and then we can sort out who's watching the donkey wheel and who's not."

Alistair quickly checked nobody was missing. "Onwards and upwards, our gang."

"Sorry I was a bit off this morning." Alistair bit into the last of his sandwiches.

"No problems. As far as I could tell, I thought you enjoyed last night as much as I did." Carly wrinkled her nose. "Keira's right; these donkeys stink. Fancy putting a picnic area next to the stables!" She chuckled and packed away the remains of her lunch.

"That's the trouble; I did enjoy it. Rather a lot in fact." He sighed as he chewed. "In fact, I'd go so far as to say it was probably the best night I've had in a long, long while."

"There's plenty more where that one came from if you'll only get down off your high horse." Carly grinned. "I'm all for seizing opportunities; carpe diem and all that."

"It's alright for you; you're young, free and single." He tore his eyes away from her breasts. "I've got a wife and three kids at home."

"So? I'm not asking you to leave them and marry me or anything. Slip away for the odd evening; tell her you're going down the working men's club or something." She shrugged and gave him a wink.

"The working men's club? Then she would know I'm having an affair!" He threw back his head and laughed.

"Okay; the tennis club or the Freemasons. Whatever's your thing; hell, I don't know."

"I've never had any hobbies. It's always been the family or work." His mind raced trying to conjure up a suitable possibility.

"You sad fucker; it's about time you had a bit on the

side." Carly stretched two light brown legs out in front of him on the grass. "No strings sex, eh? I've already got a feeling we could be well matched in the bedroom department. You don't often get that in a relationship."

Alistair longed to run his hand up the inside of her shorts. He knew she was right. She would be up for the kind of experimental sex he had often thought about, but would not even think of suggesting to Ann. Turning his eyes towards the group as they stood petting the donkeys, he exhaled forcefully.

"I had a vasectomy years ago. You won't catch a dose or get pregnant if I don't wear a condom."

"That'll save me buying them then. Same here, although I'll have my work cut out trying to knock you up." She leaned back on her hands and grinned up at the sky.

"Great; I always reckon wearing a rubber is like trying to thread a needle while you've got a pair of mittens on." His heart had already started beating faster in anticipation of the evening ahead.

"No mittens. No strings. No babies. No clap. Perfect!" Carly stood up. "Get down on it, tiger, but right now it's time to be responsible again and stop Sanderson and Lisa sloping off for a quick one instead of going on the guided tour."

CHAPTER 12

HE DOZED UNTIL Sanderson's bass tones no longer permeated through his bedroom wall. After waking himself up with a shower, he quietly locked his room, crept downstairs to the first floor, and tapped lightly on Carly's door.

"Come in, tiger." She whispered. "They've finally shut up I think."

As soon as he saw her wrapped in the flimsiest of bathrobes he felt himself beginning to stiffen. She closed the door and he drew her to him, untying her robe and sliding his hands over her breasts and then around her back.

"It feels good; don't stop." She lifted his top over his head and laid her cheek against his bare chest. "Mmmm."

Alistair, all senses sharpened by her nearness, picked up on the aroma of coconut shampoo as he rubbed his nose in her hair.

"You smell good." He sighed. "You're so beautiful: I can't get enough of you."

"I thought you were tired?" She wrapped her arms

around his waist and squeezed.

"Not anymore." He chuckled. "I can keep going all night."

"Follow me then." She clasped one hand around his throbbing penis and led him towards the bed. "Actions speak louder than words, so they say."

He kissed her deeply as they lay together, feeling his excitement mount as her tongue slid around his.

"What do you like?" His breathing quickened as he ran a hand down towards her pubic bone.

"Anything. I've done it all. I'm totally un-shockable." She smiled and rubbed herself against him. "Whatever you fancy is fine by me."

Alistair felt as excited as a teenage youth let loose in a whorehouse for the first time. Ann's expression of disgust at the only time he had ever mentioned trying anal sex would be forever imprinted on his brain.

"Turn over." He swallowed hard. "Kneel up a bit."

He wondered where the sounds of girls' voices were coming from; none of the high-pitched tones sounded at all like Jessie's. His leg lay over a warm, rounded body, whose back was pressed in against his chest, and whose hair smelt of coconut shampoo. As the sleep left his body and he realised where he was, Alistair sat up in alarm.

"Fuck! Wake up!" He shook her and whispered. "The girls are out there in the corridor!"

Carly gave a sleepy giggle.

"Cool it, tiger. I'll tell them to go back into their rooms. Can you get ready in fifteen minutes?"

"I'll have to shower here in case the boys are running about upstairs. Have you got a razor?" He threw back the duvet, jumped out of bed, and rubbed his eyes.

"No; I had a full leg and bikini wax last week." She lifted one bare and hairless leg up in the air.

"Shit. Don't get me going again. I'll use your bathroom; tell them to go back in."

"Okay, but don't stink it up. Wait 'til you go back to your own room for that." She giggled.

His heart was in his mouth as he crept back up to the second floor. With some dismay he saw that all the bedroom doors were open, with boys flitting in and out of each other's rooms. He gave a cursory nod to Michael Pritchard, as his small frame appeared in the corridor.

"Is it breakfast time yet, Sir?"

"Nearly, Pritchard. I had to walk down and buy a razor; I'll just have a quick shave and then I'll be ready.   Give me

ten minutes."

"Okay."

Alistair sighed as Pritchard disappeared again. When he was safely behind his bedroom door he gave a sigh of relief, checking in the mirror to see if his appearance could have possibly given Pritchard any food for thought. Satisfied that apart from a five o'clock shadow, his clothes were unwrinkled and his hair was neat, Alistair raked a razor over his face, cleaned his teeth, and stepped out into the corridor again.

"Come on chaps; look lively! Who wants breakfast?" He felt inordinately pleased that nobody had suspected a thing.

"We do! We were waiting for you!" Leon Tucker was first in the queue.

"Well, I'm here now. Let's get going."

Ignoring the sounds of female voices on the first floor,

Alistair led his troupe down to the dining room. As he supervised the boys waiting in line he could hear Carly chattering to the girls as they came down the stairs. His heart started beating a tattoo in his chest at the thought of her standing behind him in the buffet queue. He tried his best to banish from his mind the memories of the night before, but found to his absolute fury that his face began to redden as soon as she came into the room.

"Morning boys! 'Morning Mr Veale!" Carly appeared brisk and business-like, with her cascading locks tied back tightly into a neat ponytail.

"'Morning Miss Jessop." The boys chorused as one, while Alistair gave a cursory nod.

"Where are we going today, Sir?" Adrienne looked up at him questioningly.

"We're going to Alum Bay over at Freshwater. There's a small theme park there, with a chairlift ride down to the beach, a boat ride out to the Needles lighthouse, and demonstrations of glass-blowing. If you've got any pocket money left you'll be able to buy a souvenir glass lighthouse and fill with it with some coloured sand. When I was a kid you used to be able to chip the coloured sands away from the cliffs, but no more. Due to too much erosion you now have to buy it at the souvenir shop." He helped himself to some scrambled egg and kept his eyes on his plate.

"Chairlifts?" Jack Denbigh piped up with interest.

"Yeah, but one boy will be riding with one girl. The two boys left over, that'll be you and Sanderson, will ride with me and Miss Jessop." Alistair kept his face expressionless, whilst adding two sausages and some baked beans to his plate.

"Why?" Kevin Sanderson's face took on a sulky look.

"To ensure you're delivered back to your parents alive

on Friday afternoon."

"I'm okay going with Miss Jessop." Jack leered.

"You can come with me, Denbigh."

"Oh, but Sir!"

"Like it or lump it."

Coachloads of tourists had already started arriving by the time Alistair parked the minibus and switched off the engine. He found the heady aroma of Carly's perfume was keeping him in a permanent state of excitement, making it difficult to concentrate on anything else other than their previous night's lovemaking. Waiting until last, he followed her out of the bus and glanced at her buttocks, tight and rounded in her khaki shorts.

"You've got a lovely arse." He whispered.

"Later, tiger." Carly turned to him and grinned.

"Sir; can we go on the chairlift first?"

With a sigh of irritation Alistair found that Adrienne had held back from the group and now stood next to him as he clambered out of the bus.

"Yes, I was going to suggest that before it gets too busy." He nodded. "Let's step on it and get our tickets."

After paying at the kiosk, he shepherded the group through the turnstiles to join the queue for the chairlifts.

"I don't like heights, Sir." Gillian Lister looked down at the beach and shook her head, terrified.

"Okay, there's a way down over there." Alistair indicated towards steep steps. "But it'll take you a while. It's only about five minutes' ride on the chairlift though."

"I'll see you at the bottom." Gillian, relieved, began to

walk towards the steps.

"Pair up; one boy with one girl! Tucker, it's best that you're the one to go on your own. Denbigh; stay with me. Sanderson, you're with Miss Jessop."

"Such an honour, Kevin." Carly smiled and curtsied.

Alistair noticed how the chatter quietened down as the group shuffled to the head of the queue. He dragged his mind away from Carly to issue last-minute instructions.

"Look how people get on to the chairlift and copy them. It won't stop, but there's plenty of time to sit down. The two men you can see working over there will also help you." He pointed to two members of staff in red t-shirts aiding the slower, and those of a nervous disposition.

He held his breath as Robert Evans and Celie Ingram jumped onto a moving seat and pulled the safety bar down. Next to go were Freddie Peterson and Adrienne Draper.

"This is cool, Sir!" Adrienne's smile was radiant.

"Hold tight, Adrienne!" Alistair smiled. "Don't lift the bar up until you're at the bottom."

"Okay!"

He grinned at Carly, who winked back as she took her seat next to Kevin Sanderson. After ensuring the rest of the group had gone, Alistair turned to Jack Denbigh and smiled.

"Our turn; jump on when I say."

"Can I walk down?" Denbigh's complexion had turned rather wan.

"You'll be alright with me, Jack. Don't worry." He was surprised at the boy's sudden nervousness. "It's a piece of cake."

"I….I haven't done this before."   Denbigh, all macho posturing seemingly vanished, looked close to tears.

"Stand on those red footprints. Ready? Sit down when

the chair comes up to you. That's all there is to it." Alistair kept his voice light. "Off we go!"

As he pulled the safety bar down, Alistair took a quick glance at the boy's face as the chairlift began its steep descent. Jack was grinning from ear to ear:

"This is great, Sir! I love it!"

For just a few moments Alistair stopped thinking about Carly's backside, and with a smile of satisfaction knew that his decision to become a teacher all those years ago was still the right one.

CHAPTER 13

"WHAT'S THE NEEDLES, Sir?" Kevin Sanderson hung over the side of the boat and tried to put his hands in the water.

"Look over by the lighthouse." Alistair, his hand on Kevin's collar, hauled the boy into a sitting position and pointed out to sea. "See those three chalky rocks out there with a gap in the middle? There were four originally, but the fourth one, the tallest of them all, collapsed in the big storm of 1764. It was that fourth rock that was needle shaped, but the name stuck anyway. It's the most Western tip of the Isle of Wight."

"Is it very choppy out there, Sir?" Celie Ingram looked at Alistair worriedly.

"It can be, but it's okay today. The boat ride up to the lighthouse only takes about half an hour, and the captain will give you a brief history of the area over the megaphone in a minute."

"Have you taken your travel sickness pill?" Carly made herself comfortable next to Celie.

"Yeah." Celie pulled a face. "This thing's bobbing up

and down though."

"Boats do tend to do that, Celie." Alistair smiled. "You'll be fine as soon as we get going."

"I don't want to walk back up all those steps." Gillian looked up at the chairlift from her seat at the front of the boat. "It'll take forever."

"Come back up with us then. "Jack shrugged. "It's a piece of cake; there's nothing to it."

Alistair turned away with a smile and found a seat next to Carly as the boat chugged away from the jetty.

"How's your sea legs?" He gently teased.

"Better than yours probably." She laughed. "So don't worry about that."

The cooling breeze was refreshing on his face. Alistair relaxed for the first time that morning and enjoyed the ride up to the lighthouse. He could see the captain's small terrier dog had taken a liking to several of the group, who were rolling a ball back and forth along the deck for it to chase. The dog barked and bounced, the teenagers happily petted the dog without listening to a word of the captain's running commentary, and Alistair enjoyed a few moments of peace with Carly.

"Last night was so awesome." He whispered, but kept his gaze on the dog.

"Pretty fucking special." Carly chuckled quietly.

"I can't wait to do it again." He mumbled under his breath and sighed.

"Me too; same time, same place tonight?" She bent over and caught the dog's ball as it rolled towards them.

"I'm getting hard already." He felt his penis stiffening and crossed his legs.

"Steady on, tiger; we've got fourteen kids to entertain first." She grinned and held the ball up in the air.

"What do you say about carrying this on when we get home?" He held his breath and gave Carly a nudge with his elbow, kept his gaze on the dog, and smiled at Adrienne as she came up to retrieve the ball.

"I live on my own, but I've got a lovely king-size bed." She whispered. "I'll leave it to you to make up the excuses."

He could feel his heart thudding with excitement as the boat made its way back to the jetty. As the crew anchored the boat and Alistair marshalled his group into line, he stopped thinking about who had already slid between Carly's sheets, and instead felt that at long last he was living for the first time in his life.

"Toilets are back up in the theme park, so if nobody needs to go we can sit on the beach here and eat our lunch." Alistair looked over at the group questioningly.

"Yeah, we can wait." Leon Tucker sat down on the stones and unzipped his rucksack.

"There was a loo on the boat; we're okay." Lisa sat down next to Kevin Sanderson.

"Right; lunchtime it is, then." Alistair counted fourteen heads and sat down.

"These stones are uncomfortable." Keira grimaced and shifted her buttocks from side to side.

"Unfortunately there's not much of a beach here, but at least it's peaceful." Alistair bit into a ham and tomato sandwich. "We'll go back up in the chairlift soon and you can have a wander around the theme park and buy some souvenirs."

"Why are all those roped off, Sir?" Celie gnawed an apple and pointed towards coloured sandstone cliffs.

"It's what I was telling you all about at breakfast." Alistair wondered if everything he said was going in one ear and out the other. "When I was a boy you could chip the sand away for a keepsake, but too many tourists doing that and the wind and rain have caused the cliffs to erode."

"So, where's the sand in the theme park shop come from then?" Adrienne sipped some water from a bottle before opening her packed lunch.

"Good question, Adrienne." He nodded. "The owners use sand that has already fallen down the cliff. How many different coloured sands do you think there are?"

"Ten?" Adrienne looked up to the top of the cliffs.

"Fifteen." Robert Evans shook his head at Adrienne.

"I can only see seven." Tyler Marshall yawned.

"There are actually twenty one colours, caused by the natural mineral content in the sand. The Victorians first began selling it, and it's carried on ever since." Alistair watched Carly bite into her apple. "Up at the top of the cliffs was the Royal Needles Hotel where Marconi sent his first ever telegraphic message, but that's gone now of course. However, we still have the coloured sands." He smiled. "Eat up, our group. Who's walking back up the stairs instead of getting on the chairlift?"

He was surprised to find that not one person raised their hand.

"Have a wander around the shop. Miss Jessop and I will sit on this seat and wait for you." Alistair sat down next to Carly where he could see the exit. "Meet back here in twenty minutes or so."

As the last of the group disappeared inside the shop, Carly looked at Alistair and smiled.

"You love this place, don't you?" She rubbed the side of her leg against his.

"Not the bloody theme park, but there's some lovely walks around here." He nodded. "We could wander off the beaten track and have a good old roll in the heather." He sighed at the thought of it.

"Sounds good; we'll have to come back again one day when there's just the two of us." She nodded. "What will you tell your wife?"

"About what?"

"About why you're suddenly going to start disappearing for the odd evening or Saturday night."

"I don't know. I haven't thought that far ahead yet." He felt a pang of guilt at the sudden image of loyal, steadfast Ann sitting up in bed waiting for him to come home. "I'll go to yours after school ends; I'll just tell her I had extra marking to do."

"Tell her you joined a gym. You'll be able to do your marking, and then come to me until about half past seven?" She glanced up at him.

"Good idea; I'll tell her I want to lose some weight." He patted his middle and laughed. "It's not too far from the truth anyway.

"I'll soon get that weight off you. You'll be as knackered riding me as you would be on a rowing machine." She hooted with laughter.

"Shhh! The kids'll be out in a minute!" He giggled. "Jesus, Carly, you don't know what you're doing to me." He sighed and ached to kiss her.

"I know what I'd *like* to do to you." She waved at Adrienne. "Ah, here's your stalker. See you later." She stood up and walked towards the shop.

He was hard before she had even opened the door. He wanted to taste and devour every inch of her body; even the sight of her fully-clothed caused him to have the kind of thoughts that had not troubled him since he had been as old as Denbigh and Sanderson. When she closed the door on the outside world, he took her in his arms and rubbed his nose in her hair.

"I want you so fucking badly; you've been at arm's length all day, and I'm going to burst in a minute." He closed his eyes and exhaled into her coconut curls as she unzipped his jeans.

"Steady on, tiger; all this cussing isn't good for you." She lowered his trousers, untied her bathrobe, and rubbed herself against him. "I nipped out to the supermarket earlier." She whispered in his ear. "Do you like strawberry yoghurt?"

"Yeah, but I'm not hungry." He stepped out of his jeans, put his hands under her buttocks, and lifted her up.

"You haven't seen where I'm going to put it yet." She nibbled his earlobe and wrapped her legs around his waist. "You might change your mind in a minute."

CHAPTER 14

THIS TIME THEY had remembered to set the alarm. As Carly reached over to turn it off he realised he was drowning in her face and body; the smell and taste of her was driving every other thought out of his mind. As for strawberry yoghurt, he was unsure whether he could ever eat it again without getting a hard-on.

She flopped back onto the pillows, and pressed her back into his chest. He closed his eyes, let his head rest on top of hers, and moved his hand around to cup her breasts while feeling his erection nestling snugly in her groin.

"Last day, tiger. Quick one before you go back up?" She squeezed his penis between her thighs.

"Don't tempt me." He moved her hair from her face and nibbled her ear. "I've got to go before the boys wake up; I need a shower." He was aware that the room had an overlying aroma of coconut, strawberry, and semen. "Open the window a bit more; the cleaner will know what we've been doing in here."

"Spoilsport!" She laughed and ground her buttocks into

him in a circular motion. "Go on then, bugger off. We can catch up tonight."

With great reluctance he tore himself away from her, threw on his clothes, and crept back upstairs to the second floor. There was nothing to be heard along the corridor as he let himself into his room, sighing with relief at arriving back undetected. By the time he had showered and shaved, signs of life could be heard outside and the powerful smell of sizzling sausages and bacon had begun to permeate through the hotel. Alistair combed his hair, searched for a clean set of clothes, and put on some socks and trainers. As he came out of his room into the corridor he came face to face with a worried-looking Freddie Peterson:

"'Morning, Peterson; ready for breakfast?"

"No Sir, Tyler's thrown my shoes out of the window."

"Well, you can go and tell Marshall that unless he retrieves them, then he'll be watching everybody else when they're horse riding today." Alistair raised his voice to carry into the bedroom.

"I heard that Sir! I'm going!" Tyler Marshall, giggling, ran out into the corridor and down the stairs.

"Are we really going horse riding, Sir?" Freddie looked up happily at Alistair.

"Yes, it's the last day today as you know. Tomorrow we catch the ferry back, so we're going to Brickfields riding centre after breakfast for a bit of a treat. Hurry up and get your shoes on; I'm going down for something to eat."

"I've never ridden a horse before, Sir." Kylie Morris climbed into the minibus. "I'm nervous."

"Don't worry" Alistair smiled at her as he started up the

engine. "There's plenty of staff available to walk along with the horses. You won't be left on your own. There's the option of going for a trek through the woods, or staying inside the centre and having a lesson."

"I want to stay inside." Kylie nodded.

"And me." Celie Ingram held up her hand.

"I want to go on the trek." Oliver Stewart's head peeped around one of the back seats.

"Okay; let's have a show of hands. How many want to stay inside and have a beginner's lesson?" Alistair swivelled around in the driver's seat to see the response. "Okay; that's about half of you." He turned to Carly. "How's your horse riding, Miss Jessop?"

"I'll go on the trek, that's fine." Carly nodded.

"Right; I'll stay with the beginners, and Miss Jessop will go with the more advanced." He selected first gear and let the handbrake off. "Let's get going; make the most of the day, our gang!"

Alistair noticed a distinct lack of chatter as six teenagers caught sight of the horses inside the sawdust-strewn hall, waiting patiently by the mounting stools for their first customers of the day.

"I'm Libby, your instructor, and this is Emily, my assistant. Are all your hats on securely? Right then, which two want to be first?"

Libby looked from left to right along the line. Finally, Adrienne and Lisa tentatively put up their hands.

"We will."

"Good girls! Stand on the stools then, and hold onto the saddle. Put your left leg in the stirrup, and swing your right leg over."

Alistair wanted to chuckle at the expressions on the girls' faces, and turned away to hide his mirth. Out of the window he could see the others mounting up. He was rather surprised to notice that Carly seemed quite at home in the saddle, and walked her horse expertly to the back of the group. He caught her eye and winked, and she gave him a grin as they all set off:

Lucky old saddle. He thought, whilst gazing at her groin.

He was pleased to see Leon Tucker given the biggest, sturdiest horse. The boy showed no sign of fear, and walked the horse around the hall with Emily holding onto the reins. Pretty soon all six teenagers had performed two laps, and after dismounting, stood together chattering excitedly.

"Now then boys and girls, before you mount up again I think Sir ought to have a go. What do you think?" Libby held the reins of the biggest horse and looked enquiringly at Alistair, whose outwardly composed demeanour suddenly evaporated:

"Oh no, I'm fine thanks." Alistair brought to mind his one and only disastrous time astride a horse and shook his head.

"Yeah, go on Sir!" Leon Tucker shouted. "I had to do it!"

"Yeah! Yeah!" Four girls clapped and cheered in unison.

"You can do it Sir!" Michael Pritchard added his voice to the others.

He could see there was nothing for it but to comply. Flashing the group a less-than-confident smile, Alistair strapped on a hard hat, swung his leg over the saddle, and hoped the torture would soon come to an end. By the time he had completed the regulation two laps, all six teenagers were jumping up and down noisily. However, after enduring fifteen minutes of absolute hell, Alistair decided that taking his age, creaky joints and initial distaste into consideration, his second horse riding lesson had actually not gone too badly at all.

"Oh, I can't open my legs; it hurts too much!" Carly squealed with laughter and curled up in a ball on the bed. "It's been ages since I've ridden a horse!"

"I don't like the sound of that." Alistair giggled and massaged her bare buttocks. "How's this? Any better?" He carried on with rhythmic stroking.

"Mmmm; don't stop." She turned over onto her front. "I'm saddle sore; you'll have to stick it somewhere else tonight."

"Whereabouts do you suggest?" His fingers ran down the cleft between her buttocks.

"To be quite honest Ali, I don't care, so long as it's not in *me*. I've got a period coming in a few days, and I'm bunged up. I'm sore and achy, and I just want a cuddle." Carly closed her eyes and yawned.

"Oh, sorry. Sure, I can do cuddles too."

Trying not to let his disappointment show, Alistair wrapped his arms around her and pulled her close to his chest. Within minutes her breathing settled, becoming slow and heavy. He rested his chin on the top of her head and savoured the sweetness of the moment. Some time later when she turned over in her sleep, he gently eased himself out of bed without waking her, dressed quickly, and crept back up to the second floor.

CHAPTER 15

"I'LL BE COMING in to check all the rooms when I've finished my own packing." Alistair stood in the back of the queue for the breakfast buffet. "We'll be leaving at eleven o'clock to catch the mid-day ferry."

"Okay." Jack Denbigh yawned and helped himself to sausages and bacon.

"Can't we stay a bit longer, Sir?" Michael Pritchard turned around to look at Alistair in the queue.

"No; it's time to go home, Pritchard." He felt the same keen disappointment as the boy. "I'll organise another trip for next year though."

"'Morning all!" Carly ushered in six miserable-looking teenage girls.

"'Morning Miss Jessop. Your group are quiet today!" Alistair let the girls go in front of him in the queue in order to take advantage of an opportunity to stand next to Carly. "What's going on?"

"We don't want to go home." Adrienne Draper stated in a sulky tone.

"It's nice to know you've all had a good time." Alistair smiled. "If your parents are happy to pay next year, then we'll do it all again."

"My mum's only too pleased to get rid of me." Keira Trelawny nodded.

"I'm sure that's not true, Keira." Carly took a plate. "Help yourself to breakfast, girls."

Alistair spooned some baked beans onto his plate and then put some bread in the toaster. Carly picked up a slice from a wholemeal loaf, and came over to stand next to him:

"I didn't even hear you go last night." She whispered and added her slice of bread to the toaster. "I was zonked; sorry."

"That's okay. I know all about periods; I've got a wife, remember?" He chuckled quietly.

"I'm a pig for a couple of days before; you'll get used to it."

"I'm used to it already. I've also got a thirteen year old daughter; now she's starting to get moody as well."

"You poor thing! Let's hope the three of us don't all come on at the same time." She snorted and took her toast. "Otherwise you'll be putting your head in the microwave."

He refrained from the temptation to put his arm around her as they stood on the upper deck of the ferry, watching the cars still driving on underneath.

"It's been a great week; I'm going to miss our nightly trysts." He smiled and looked up at a circling seagull. "Although I could do without the fourteen kids." He glanced quickly over his shoulder to check the teenagers were all still seated and checking their phones.

"Tryst? Is that what they call it?   I thought it was lust!"

She whispered and gave him a nudge. "Don't forget the king-size bed at mine."

"How could I forget? I'll be in it as soon as I'm able to." He sighed and watched the crew making last-minute preparations for sailing.

"This time next week my period will be over. Give me your phone and I'll put my number on it, and then you can do the same for mine." She took the iPhone from him. "I'll put my name down as Albert, and then your wife won't suspect anything. I'll send you a message and let you know when to come over." She tapped away on the phone's keyboard. "I'll never send you any compromising texts, so don't worry." She passed him her phone.

"Cheers for that." He sighed again and tapped in his phone number. "There's one question I need to ask you." He looked down and shuffled awkwardly.

"Get it over with then." She grinned and looked at him.

"Who's Barry? You mentioned earlier in the week that Barry could give you a lift home."

"He's my brother, you dickhead. You've got the job today; I haven't phoned him."

As the ferry set sail he slipped Carly back her phone and followed her over to the seating area. He felt as miserable as the teenagers looked, although somewhat pleased to know Barry's identity and that their affair would not be coming to an end. Although only a week had gone by, he knew he would find it hard to be without her. She had taken over all his waking thoughts, and as he looked at her russet curls blowing around her face in the breeze he knew without a doubt that he loved her with an all-encompassing passion he had never felt for anyone before.

"Come in to my humble abode. Don't worry; there's nobody else living here." She unlocked the front door, took his hand, and led him into a dark vermilion hallway. "It sucks, I know; Barry did it with a job load of paint he'd nicked." She laughed.

"It's different, I'll give it that." Alistair looked around. "I quite like it actually; it's you." He nodded.

"That's what Barry said. Cup of coffee?" She threw her rucksack and keys on the floor and put her arms around him.

"In a minute; I just want to feel your body against mine." He pressed her close to him and closed his eyes.

"My period started early; as long as that's all you want to do." She looked up at him.

"Yeah; I'd love to do more, but only if you're willing." He laughed and sank his face in her hair. "God; I love you so much."

"You're not supposed to say that, tiger." She gave him a squeeze. "No strings, remember?"

"I know what I said, but I can't help it." He sighed. "I can't stop thinking about you."

He cupped her chin with his hands and kissed her open mouth, letting his tongue mingle pleasantly with hers. When her hand wriggled down the front of his shorts he kissed her more deeply. She pulled away from him and took his hand again.

"Come upstairs; I want to give you something to keep you going for a few days."

"I thought you said…..?" He looked at her questioningly.

"I want to give *you* something. You're not listening!" She led him to the staircase.

"I am; believe me I am." He laughed; his confined erection already uncomfortable.

He passed more vermilion walls on the upstairs landing, with framed family photos dotted about haphazardly. As she led him into the front bedroom and pulled down the blind, he took in the textured black wallpaper, black fluffy carpet, and midnight blue quilt complete with silver moons and stars.

"Jeez! Black walls?" He shook his head in wonder.

"Yeah, I like it that way." She unzipped his shorts. "Come on."

He took off his clothes and lay on the bed, his heart thudding excitedly in his chest. He watched as she pulled her t-shirt over her head, unhooked her bra, and straddled his legs.

"Don't move a muscle." She bent forwards and ran her tongue along the length of his penis. "You're going to like this."

CHAPTER 16

TRYING DESPERATELY TO shake off the growing feeling of despondency, he brought the minibus to rest on his driveway, turned off the engine and opened the door. Within seconds a mini whirlwind had thrown itself at him.

"Daddy!" Jessie flung her arms around him. "I've missed you so much!"

"I've missed you too, darling." Alistair laughed and gave her a squeeze. "How's school been?"

"Horrible; I'm glad there's only another week to go".

"You've done really well. Mummy and I are very proud of you." He kissed the top of her head.

"I love you, Daddy."

"I love you too. Are you still my princess?"

"Yeah."

Strangely enough he suddenly wanted to sob as he held his daughter. Out of the corner of his eye he could see Ann standing in the doorway, neat and well-presented as always. With one arm around Jessie, he fought back tears, picked up his rucksack, and walked towards his wife.

"Hello darling; sorry I'm late. We missed the ferry and had to wait for another one." The lie slipped out easily as he kissed her briefly on the cheek. "It's good to be home."

"Have you had dinner?" Ann took the rucksack from him. "There's some stew left over from yesterday, but we've had ours."

"Lovely; I'm starving. The stew sounds great." He took off his trainers. "Where are the boys?"

"Jake's at youth club, and Tom I think is out with a *girl*." Ann chuckled. "He was very cagey tonight about where he was going."

"Well, he's at the right age for it. I'll pick Jake up later on if you like. You'll need to give me a lift home from school tomorrow after I've dropped the minibus off."

"Of course."

He gave Jessie another kiss and followed Ann into the kitchen, noticing how she had already started to sort through the rucksack and bring out items for the laundry. He opened the fridge and took out a beer, trying not to appear the least bit bothered about any semen stains that might be visible on his underpants.

"Jess; what have you been up to all week?" He sat down at the table, kept one eye on his wife, and opened the can.

"Homework, swimming club and fighting with Jake." Jessie shrugged. "Same as always. Where have you been?"

"Back to the island with some of my tutor group. We visited Osborne, Carisbrooke Castle, Alum Bay, and Brickfields riding school." He downed half the can in one go as he tried to banish the mental image of Carly astride a chestnut mare.

"Oh, you've never taken me to Brickfields!" Jessie whined. "That's not fair!"

"Jessie, don't start." Ann glared at her daughter. "Daddy's only just got in."

"We can go next time we visit." Alistair smiled. "Let me have something to eat and then we can play a game or something before I have to go out and pick Jake up."

"Okay; I'll be upstairs in my room."

The stew was nutritious and tasty, as he knew it would be. The house was clean and well-kept, just as he expected. However, when he looked at Ann there was no fire burning in his belly and groin. Twenty years of marriage had dulled the flames of lust to the weakest of smouldering embers, and Alistair realised he needed those fires in his life again to feel like a real man. Carly had lit the touch paper, but she had not stood well back. She had warmed his body with her own fiery magnetism; the heat between them that afternoon had been so intense that she had brought him to juddering orgasm almost immediately. As he speared a piece of beef with his fork he remembered the shape of her breasts as she straddled his legs, and the way her tongue would flick along the shaft of his penis towards the tip and then back again. To even suggest that Ann might want to do the same thing would be akin to asking her to fly to the moon. He sighed and rubbed a hand over his eyes.

"Not hungry? You haven't eaten much." Ann collected his plate and discarded cutlery. "Did you eat on the ferry?"

"Yeah, I had a sandwich. I'm just a bit tired that's all; it's been a long drive."

"Don't worry; I'll get Jake. You have a nice bath and an early night." She smiled at him as she washed up his plate. "Take Madam off my hands for an hour or two though if you can; she's been driving me mad this week."

"Okay: I'll go up to her now." He stood up, glad for an excuse to be out of the kitchen.

"She's got homework I think. She was waiting for you to come in and help her with it."

"Will do." He gave her a thumbs up as he made his way to the stairs.

"Hi Jess, can I come in?"

Alistair tapped lightly on the bedroom door, which was opened almost immediately:

"Daddy, can you help me with my homework please?" Jessie waved an exercise book in the air.

"What homework is it?" Alistair's heart sank at the thought of it.

"Science; it's so *boring*. It's about the law of the lever and something to do with fulcrums and some old man called Archimedes. I don't want to do it." Jessie pouted.

"Lots of things in life have to be done even though we don't want to do them, and Science homework comes under that heading." Alistair thought he sounded like an old worn out gramophone record. "We'll look it up together on Google, and then we can play one of your computer games afterwards if you like."

"Thanks! I'm so glad you're home!"

He gave her a hug and she grinned at him. Alistair suddenly experienced a momentary *frisson* of guilt that he had hardly thought about his wife, daughter or two sons at all during his entire week away.

"Are you staying downstairs to wait up for Tom?" Alistair popped his head around the living room door, hopeful that he might be able to go to bed undisturbed.

"No, I'll come up now. He's got a key; he'll phone if he needs us I'm sure."

Ann switched off the TV, plunging the room into silence. Alistair made his way upstairs, unable to shake off a feeling of gloom that had crept over him. As he donned his usual pyjama bottoms and slid underneath the duvet he tried to shut out the agreeable sensation of lying naked with Carly's back pressed against his chest.

Next door in the bathroom was the sound of an electric toothbrush. Eyes closed, he lay flaccid and impotent, waiting for the moment when he would have to show a modicum of excitement at being back in the marital bed. When the bedroom door opened he willed himself to open his eyes and turn towards his wife.

"Have you left the porch light on for Tom?" He knew the answer already, but could not think of anything else to say.

"Yes. He didn't come in until after midnight last Sunday." She climbed in beside him. "He doesn't seem to care if it's college the next day or not."

"Neither did I at his age. He's had all the lectures. We have to let him grow up and do his thing."

He put an arm around Ann's shoulder, but the action felt wooden and contrived. She sighed as she put her head on his chest:

"I hate going to bed knowing he's not home."

"The phone's here by the bed. He'll ring if he needs us; don't worry." He gave her shoulder a squeeze.

"I've missed you this week."   Ann looked up at him.

"What's Carly like? What do you think of her?"

"She's okay; I'm glad to be home though." He hoped his smile appeared genuine.

"Do you like my new nightie?" She lifted up the duvet. "I bought it today."

"It's great." He ran a hand down the front of a billowing neck to ankle creation that would not have looked out of place on his grandmother. "Sexy."

"My boobs are a bit sore; sorry." She brought one arm up protectively across her bosom.

"That's okay." He sighed with relief. "I'm knackered anyway."

CHAPTER 17

"HEY, TOM. Good night out?"

Alistair looked up from eating his lunch, noticing with surprise a large love bite on the side of his son's neck.

"Great, thanks." Tom yawned and scratched his bare chest. "Is it lunch time already?"

"Yeah; you've missed breakfast." Jessie cut her slice of pizza into dainty squares. "You need a shower."

"Yes, little sister. I'll just get some coffee and then comply with your wishes." Tom poked his tongue out at Jessie.

"Did you know you've got a hickey?" Jake crammed a forkful of pasta into his mouth and pointed a finger at his brother's neck.

"Cheers." Tom's face reddened as he turned away towards the kettle.

"What's a hickey?" Jessie looked at Jake.

"Never you mind." Ann looked sternly at her daughter. "Tom, can you go and get dressed, please. It's one o'clock in the afternoon."

"I'm going, I'm going. Save me a bit of pizza." Tom spooned some coffee in a mug and poured out some boiling water. "Don't let Jake eat it all."

"I'll do you some sandwiches for when you've had a wash." Ann put down her knife and fork. "But you can't eat lunch in your pyjama trousers."

"I don't need dinner tonight, I'm going down to Yarmouth with some mates after work and staying over; be back Sunday night." Tom paused briefly by the kitchen door.

"Staying over where?" Ann glanced up at him.

"We're kipping in Terry's car; it's all cool. Don't worry." Tom sauntered up the hallway.

"Can I go with you?" Jake piped up hopefully.

"In your dreams, little brother."

"Ali, you need to speak to Tom before he goes to work." Ann rubbed a plate clean rather too vigorously. "I don't like the sound of it."

"I will do if it'll make you feel better, but he's a young lad that needs to do the things young lads do." Alistair picked up the plate for drying. "I've done it too at his age."

"Done what?" Ann looked at him inquisitively.

"Spent the weekend at Yarmouth, and pissed all my money up the wall."

"Charming."

"Let him loose, Ann. He's not a bad lad. Let him go." Alistair shrugged and checked his phone for messages. "We're here to pick up the pieces if it all goes tits up."

"Well, just remind him about drugs and STD's."

"I'm sure he knows; we've drummed it into him since he was Jessie's age."

"Go on, do it now. He's had his lunch; he'll be going to work in a minute. Oh, and we've also got to take Jessie to Sarah's for a sleepover."

Alistair climbed the stairs and tapped lightly on his son's bedroom door:

"Yeah?"

He opened the door and smiled at Tom, who was busy packing a rucksack:

"Everything going okay?" He suddenly wished he was seventeen again.

"Great thanks!" Tom gave him a thumbs up.

"Er….Mum's a bit concerned regarding your sleeping arrangements tonight."

"How about you?" Tom winked. "What do you think?"

"I've told her that you've had all the lectures and that you're a sensible lad." Alistair chuckled, keeping his voice light.

"You can give me another little talk if you like. Let's see, what one shall we have? Sex? Drugs? STD's? Making sure that Terry only drives at twenty eight miles an hour?" Tom laughed, pulled the sides of the rucksack together, and zipped it up.

"All I'll say is make sure you're using a condom, son. It's safer that way."

"I'm her first boyfriend. She's a virgin." Tom looked at his father as he put his bank card and loose change in his back pocket.

"Not any more by the sound of it. Take my advice; it's better to put a glove on it until you find out a little bit more about her."

"But….."

"They all say they're virgins, Tom; it's what blokes want to hear." Alistair sighed. "Never underestimate a woman; they'll do everything in their power to get what they want."

"Clare's not like that." Tom shook his head.

"Okay, but don't say I haven't warned you." Alistair shrugged. "Look after yourself."

"Cheers." Tom slapped his father's hand with his own. "I'm off to cook burgers now, and then……Yarmouth!"

"See you tomorrow." Alistair smiled. "Try and come back with some money."

As he came out of his son's room, he saw Jake coming up the stairs.

"Dad, can I have a lift to Stephen's? His mum says I can come for tea."

"Sure. I've got to take the minibus back to school, but I'll drop you off on the way." Alistair checked his phone for messages. "I'll just see if Mum's ready; she's giving me a lift back."

"Yes, I heard you! I'm ready." Ann picked up her bag. "Jessie! Come on, we'll take you to Sarah's as well.   Tom…. lock up when you go out!"

"Sarah's mum will bring me back." Jessie picked up her overnight bag. "Can I ride in the minibus, Dad?"

"Come on then; Dad's taxi service is at your convenience."

"I'm going in the front." Jake towered over his sister.

"No; actually *I* am." Jessie stated her case calmly.

"*Actually*, neither of you are."   Alistair sighed and checked his phone again. "You can both get in the back."

"Are you expecting a message from somebody?" Ann asked. "You keep looking at your phone."

"Oh, no." Alistair shook his head and smiled. "It's just a habit."

He was loathe to leave the minibus, still holding pleasant memories and a faint aroma of Carly's perfume. Smiling at Ann through the windscreen as she sat watching him in the car, he climbed out and locked the door, but then felt the iPhone vibrate in his pocket. He held up the palm of his hand towards Ann and unlocked the driver's door again, turning away from her and walking to the back of the bus. With a rapidly beating heart he sat on a seat and quickly pulled the phone from his pocket, glancing at the message.

'It's Albert; Wednesday after work?'

A smile spread over his features as he tapped a grinning emoticon showing white teeth as big as tombstones. As he sent the message a voice at the door made him jump.

"What are you doing?" Ann climbed up into the bus.

"Just checking nobody left anything behind." He stood up and followed her out. "Can we stop at the gym on the way home?"

"The gym? Why?" She looked at him in puzzlement.

"I want to join up. Walking round with all those teenagers last week I realised I'm out of shape. I need to lose a bit of weight and change my fat to muscle."

"Good idea; perhaps I'll join you." Ann laughed.

"I think I'll go a couple of times a week after work. In that way I won't be home too late."

"Oh, that time's no good for me." She shook her head. "Perhaps I'll sign up for a few classes in the mornings."

"Great; we'll both be as fit as fleas then."

He smiled at her and heaved a sigh of relief. *He would let her see him go in and collect an application form, but she would never find out that he had no intention of ever signing up. Why spend thirty pounds every month to go to a gym he would never use, when he could perform a rather more pleasant variation, horizontal jogging, in Carly's black bedroom?*

CHAPTER 18

ALISTAIR KICKED CARLY'S front door shut with his foot, and wrapped his arms around her.

"God; I've been aching to hold you!" He inhaled her scent and closed his eyes in ecstasy.

"Steady on tiger, don't blow a gasket!" She laughed. "I've made you a sex pie, so come and eat first."

"A sex pie? What's that?" He kissed her hungrily. "I'm supposed to be at the bloody gym! She'll have my dinner ready when I get home. If I start eating here as well I'll be twice the size in no time."

"Ah, but this is Carly's sex pie; it contains superfoods that put the lead in your pencil. My tiger will be no good without any lead in his pencil." She reached down and caressed the bulge in his trousers. "Fancy a bit?"

"I fancy a lot, but I'll have a little bit of sex pie first." He slapped her behind gently and roamed his hands over her body. "Hurry up, before this tiger pops his cork."

He followed her into the kitchen where the delicious aroma of pastry caused him to salivate as it assailed his nostrils. Already laid on the table were two small plates, two forks, two glasses of wine, and a steaming pie in the middle of the table which had been placed on a cork mat. Chopin's Nocturne in e flat major wafted peacefully through the speakers of a CD player perched on a high shelf.

"You feed some to me, and I'll do the same for you." She took a seat, cut a piece of pie and put it on one of the plates. "Sit down; are you ready?" She ran her tongue around her lips. "Open your mouth and close your eyes."

"That's the best offer I've had all day." Alistair snorted with laughter. "I can't wait!"

The tang of apricots, cherries and peaches slid tantalisingly over his taste buds, and he chewed with relish. A further forkful was followed by a welcome sip of cold Riesling, which only seemed to accentuate the taste of the fruit. Starved of sight, his whole mouth was alive with sensation, and welcomed the feel of her tongue sliding in and out between mouthfuls over a background of Chopin's melodic crescendos.

"Carly, I can't hold out much longer." He swallowed a luscious peach and exhaled forcefully.

"Feed me, then." She commanded. "I need some sex pie too."

He opened his eyes, picked a slice of kiwi up with his fork, and placed it in her mouth. He could see that she was bra-less, and he ran his hand under her t-shirt and caressed her nipples as she chewed. He kissed her open mouth greedily, before placing half an apricot soaked in juice on her tongue.

"How's that?"

"Mmm; lovely." She chewed slowly, enjoying the flavour. "How do you like my sex pie?"

"It's pretty hot." He ran a hand under her skirt. "Have you lost your underwear?"

"Yeah." She opened her legs. "Do you mind?"

"Not in the least." Placing a cherry in her mouth, he picked her up and carried her upstairs to the black bedroom.

"You've been ages. I tried to call you, but I assume you had no signal at the gym?"

Ann, in her dressing gown and slightly irritated, opened his car door before he had even switched off the engine.

"I turned it off and locked it away with my clothes. I can't pump iron and talk on the phone at the same time."

"I thought you were only going for an hour."

His wife's voice was definitely disapproving. Alistair, his mind distracted by sex pie and the velvety warmth of Carly's vagina, checked his watch to find that nearly four hours had seemingly fled to the four corners of the earth.

"Sorry; I got a bit carried away. I'm absolutely starving." He stepped out of the car. "I won't be so long next time."

"Jake needs picking up from youth club in ten minutes, and Jessie's asleep. I was trying to phone you to make sure you remembered."

"Can you go? I need to have something to eat." "I'm in my nightclothes now; I've just had a bath." "Shit; okay I'll do it." He *tutted* with annoyance and started up the engine.

"You *always* pick him up. Why did you forget tonight?"

"It won't happen again; I'm going now."

Not even waiting for her to move out of the way, he put the car in reverse gear and backed out of the driveway. He felt tired, hungry, and dismayed at how his wonderful evening had deteriorated in such a short space of time. As he pulled up outside the youth club he was surprised to see the building was in darkness and that his son was hanging about outside on his own.

"Where's everybody?" Alistair opened the car's passenger door.

"They closed up half an hour ago. I tried to let you know but your phone was switched off, and Mum didn't answer." Jake jumped in the car and yawned.

"Sorry; I was at the gym and Mum was in the bath." "It's okay; I knew you'd be along at half past nine as usual."

Alistair felt waves of guilt wash over him. He had not remembered at all. While Carly had been bringing him to orgasm for the third and final time, his son had been standing outside a darkened youth club all on his own. He smiled at Jake, suddenly knowing how to make amends.

"Do you fancy some fish and chips? The shop's still open."

"Yeah! I spent all my money tonight on sweets."

"Shut the door then; let's go."

A heavenly aroma of frying potatoes enveloped him as Alistair opened the door of the fish and chip shop. There were no other customers, and soon he was sitting in the car with Jake enjoying battered cod and chips, wrapped in paper, and smothered in salt and vinegar.

"Thanks Dad, this is lovely!" Jake smiled showing a mouthful of chips.

"Yeah; I'm famished." Alistair chewed quickly. "We'll have to do this more often."

"Every Wednesday?" Piped up Jake hopefully.

"Yeah; it can be our little treat." Alistair picked up some

hot batter. "Just don't tell your mum."

"Your dinner's in the microwave." Ann came down the stairs as Alistair unlocked the front door. "Give it three minutes on full power."

"Okay; you go to bed; I'll be up in a minute. Jake, teeth and bed; it's still a school day tomorrow." Alistair ruffled the top of his son's head.

"Night, Dad."

"See you tomorrow."

When his wife and son had gone upstairs, Alistair took his dinner out of the microwave and flushed it down the toilet.

CHAPTER 19

THE LAST DAY of term always held mixed feelings for him. On one hand six weeks of freedom loomed before him, but then on the other hand the troublemakers in his tutor group would be either moving on or leaving, and there was always the feeling of trepidation as the new term began until he was sure that nobody worse had taken their place. As Alistair sat at his desk on that last day he mused that now there was an added disappointment; he would not be able to see Carly every day until the beginning of September.

When the bell went for the end of lessons, the children were out of the door like a stampeding herd of elephants. As he collected his things together he was surprised when Adrienne Draper popped her head around the door.

"Bye Sir; see you in September." She smiled. "I don't think I'll be in your group anymore, but I'll still see you around."

"Sure, Adrienne. Have a good summer." He waved to her as she closed the door and disappeared.

True to form, when the coast was clear, the one he had

been hanging back for opened the classroom door:

"All clear, tiger?" Carly looked up and down the corridor before coming into the room.

"Yeah, they've all buggered off thank God." He sighed and leaned back in his chair.

"Are we on for tomorrow night?" She perched on the end of his desk; her skirt riding up to reveal a knee and part of her thigh.

"No, it's Saturday." He resisted the temptation to put his hand on her leg. "Ann's got us tickets for some poxy concert." He yawned. "What about Monday and Thursday evenings?"

"Okay. I'll be off to see my sister in Detroit the week after next for a fortnight, so we'd better make the most of it on Thursday night." She winked at him.

"Make me some more sex pie." He reached out to hold her hand but then stopped mid-way. "God, I'm going to miss you."

"Me too. I always go at this time of year though." She sighed. "The tickets have been booked for ages."

"These past few weeks with you have taught me something, apart from how to perform anal sex to give both of us the same amount of pleasure." He looked away from her thigh and focused his gaze out of the window.

"What?" She guffawed.

"That I don't want to be with Ann anymore; I want to be with you."

There; he had said it. The feelings he could no longer ignore were out in the open.

"I never wanted to be a home wrecker." Carly whispered. "But we're good for each other. I'm on your wavelength; you're on mine; it feels right." She nodded.

"It does; I knew it even on the island. My marriage is all but dead; dead as a fucking dodo." He felt tears start at the back of his eyes. "I don't want to go home, Carly, but if I leave my kids will hate me."

"Take the time while I'm away to talk to your wife and kids. You can move in with me any time you like. My bed is empty without you." She ruffled his hair. "Cheer up, tiger. It'll all work itself out."

"It won't; not unless I make the first move and pluck up the courage to change my life."

"Do it when you're ready; I'll be waiting. I love you, Ali."

"I love you too." He put his head in his hands and sighed.

As he climaxed inside her on their last Thursday evening he wished that time could stand still, that his children always loved him, that the woman he adored would not go to Detroit, and for himself to remain forever there in the black bedroom with her safe in his arms.

"I love you so much, darling." He kissed her deeply and flopped down on top of her, running his hands down her body. "I'm missing you already."

"This is the first year that I don't want to go to the States." She smiled at him and ran her fingernails up and down his back. "Get off, tiger, you're heavy; let me lay on top of you."

He rolled off her and lay on his back, pulling her up onto his chest and running his fingers through her hair.

"I've got a key cut for you. If it all gets nasty while I'm away, you can move in here." She raised her head and looked up at him. "I'll give it to you before you go."

"I don't want to go; I don't want you to go." He sighed.

"Next year you can come with me. You'll love Caron; she's a hoot."

"I can imagine the two of you discussing me; it's a good thing I'm *not* there." He grinned.

"Girl talk. You'll get to know Howard; he's okay. They've got one son, David, who I spoil rotten." She laughed and nuzzled her face in his chest.

"Aunties are supposed to do that." He thought of his own three children without a father to spoil them. "I'm going to speak to Ann tonight. I can't go on like this; it's not fair to Ann or the kids, and it's not fair to you."

"We're right together, tiger. You know it as much as I do." She kissed him tenderly. "I love you more than I've ever loved anyone before; remember that."

"I will." He wrapped his arms around her. "Come back safe to me."

He looked at his face in the mirror as he cleaned his teeth. His features seemed drawn, and more worry lines were appearing on his forehead. Alistair sighed as he rinsed his mouth, and was suddenly aware of somebody standing at the bathroom door.

"I've signed up for a step class at your gym." Ann, clad in her new nightdress that he hated so much, brushed her hair and gazed at him.

"That's nice." He wiped his mouth on a towel.

"I opened the bank statement today by mistake. I couldn't help but notice that there's no direct debit going to Fitter Bodies. How are you paying them?"

"Ah yes; I need to speak to you about that." He felt sick inside and his heart started thudding. "I've finished in here; come to bed if you're ready."

He pulled back the duvet with trembling hands, aware that now there was no going back, and that his life was about to alter irretrievably. He watched with dread as his wife closed the door and turned on the bedside lamp.

"What do you need to speak to me about?"

He turned as if in slow motion to see Ann taking off her slippers and climbing into bed beside him. He sat up and hugged his knees, not wanting to look at her:

"Er…. I haven't actually been going to the gym." He put his head down on his knees and waited for the inevitable response.

"Where have you been then? You've been going out twice a week, sometimes three times, for weeks now."

He felt physically sick; the food he had eaten earlier was now lying like cement in his stomach.

"There's no easy way to tell you this. I've found somebody else." He turned towards her. "I'm so sorry."

He wanted to hold her tight as her face crumpled before him, and knew he would remember her expression at that moment in time for as long as he lived.

"You bastard! You lying, scheming bastard! How could you do this to me?" She climbed out of bed again and stood looking down at him, tears already filling her eyes. "I've sacrificed my career to bring up your children, and now you want to run off with somebody else? It's her, Carly, isn't it? Don't deny it!"

"I'm sorry; I'm sorry. I can't help my feelings." He nodded. "You're right; it happened while we were on the island. I'll see that you're well looked after. You keep the house and your car. I'll only take some clothes and my own car and I'll pay for whatever you and the kids need, but I can't let her go." He fought hard to keep his voice from breaking. "I have to be with her."

"Then you can get out of my bed!" Ann pointed towards the door. "Take a spare blanket and sleep on the settee. I don't want you anywhere near me! We'll tell the children tomorrow."

"I'll tell them. I don't want them to hate me." On the verge of tears, he climbed out of bed. "This has got nothing to do with them."

Feeling sicker than ever, but somewhat relieved that his secret was out in the open, Alistair grabbed a blanket and pillow from the wardrobe. As he opened the bedroom door, incessant waves of nausea overcame him. He ran to the bathroom and retched until his stomach was empty.

CHAPTER 20

HE GAVE UP trying to sleep after 2am, and just sat on the settee turning everything over in his mind. At 6.30am he heard Tom's alarm sounding and a pile of newspapers being thrown into the porch for his son to deliver. Alistair stood up, brought the stack of papers into the kitchen, and switched the kettle on.

"You're up early for school holidays." Tom yawned as he came into the room. "You look terrible, Dad. Are you alright?"

"Not really." Alistair sighed, knowing what he had to do. "I have some bad news for you, but it will never affect the way I feel about you and your brother and sister."

"What's up?" Tom, wide awake now, gazed at his father.

"Your mother and I are separating. I'm so sorry, but I needed to tell you as soon as possible."

He watched his son sit down, open-mouthed with shock:

"You're joking, right?" Tom asked hopefully.

"I'm afraid not. I've found somebody else, but as I said before, I love you, Jake and Jessie just the same. It's just that

I can't live with Mum anymore."

"Christ, Dad; I don't know what to say." Tom's eyes were watery and his voice husky. "This is terrible."

"I'm so sorry. All I can say is, the way you feel about Clare is the way I feel about Carly. I didn't think this would ever happen to me, but it has." Alistair reached out his arms to Tom. "Don't hate me for it; I feel bad enough about myself as it is for breaking up the home."

As Tom rushed into his arms Alistair lost control of his emotions. Tears coursed down his cheeks as he hugged his son close to him:

"I'm so very sorry, son. I just can't give her up."

"I don't hate you; I just don't know what to do!" Tom sobbed.

"There's nothing *to* do. Come and visit me anytime you want. I'll give you the address where I'll be. You'll always be welcome."

He pulled away, wiped his eyes, and found a pen. Tearing off a piece of scrap paper he wrote down Carly's address and gave it to Tom:

"Here; keep it safe. Bring your sister and brother anytime. I'll be going there today after I've packed a few things. You know my mobile number; I'll always keep my phone switched on just in case you want to chat."

"I've got to deliver these papers now." Tom blew his nose and took the address. "Will you still be here when I get back?"

"Probably. I need to speak to Jake and Jessie first. They need to hear it from me and not your mother." Alistair reached for two mugs out of the cupboard, added coffee and hot water from the kettle, and poured in a dash of milk. "Here; have this." He handed a mug to Tom.

"I'll go and get Jake now. He said he wanted to help me deliver the papers for a bit of money today." Tom exhaled a shaky breath and took the mug of coffee. "God knows how Jessie's going to take it." He began to walk back towards the door.

"She won't wake up until about eight o'clock." Alistair sipped his coffee. "I'll be here when she does."

He flopped down, spent, on a kitchen stool, and waited to do it all over again. When he heard footsteps coming down the stairs he stood up, heart beating fast:

"Tom's getting dressed. He says you've got something to tell me." Jake, clad in jeans and t-shirt, looked suspiciously at Alistair.

"I don't often ask for this, but I really need a hug, son." Alistair, fresh tears filling his eyes, held out his hands.

"Why?" Jake, standing his ground, looked quizzically at his father.

"Because I don't want you to hate me." Alistair wiped his eyes and lowered his arms. "Your mother and I are going to separate, but that doesn't mean that I don't love you or your brother and sister."

"You're not going to live here anymore?" Jake, aghast, stared at his father.

"No, I'm afraid not, because I've found somebody else. I've given Tom my new address, and you'll be welcome to visit any time. My phone will always be switched on in case you want to chat. I love you just the same as I always have, but I have to live with Carly now."

Alistair held out his arms once more as, devastated, Jake began to cry. He walked forward and took his son in his arms as Tom ran back down the stairs, holding out one arm in order to embrace them both.

"So sorry, boys, for doing this to you."

"Steven's dad has gone as well." Jake sniffed.

"I haven't gone, Jake. Remember that. Tom has my address. I'm less than ten minutes' drive away, or about half an hour if you and your brother want to cycle over. I'd be very happy to see you anytime." He felt a great sense of relief that the boys had not shunned him. "I have to move there today, but I'm never going to lose touch with you. Would you like me to help you with the papers today? I can take you round in the car if you like?"

"Okay; thanks." Tom nodded. "You probably need to be out of the house as much as possible today. He laughed weakly. "I assume you're not Mum's favourite person?"

"You could say that, but who can blame her? I just need to speak to Jessie when I get back. Let's go now then; we'll be done in half an hour and we can have breakfast when we get back. I'll just go and get dressed first."

Just like a normal day, the smell of frying bacon made his mouth water as Alistair came in through the front door with Tom and Jake. Ann was in the kitchen, but he noticed that she did not turn around as he followed the boys towards the smell of food.

"Tom and Jake, there's bacon rolls on the table there for you." Ann wiped her hands on a piece of kitchen paper. "Ali, I'm assuming that *she's* cooking you some breakfast this morning, so you'd best hurry up and get back there."

"I will do, but I need to speak to Jessie first." Alistair ignored his rumbling stomach.

"I've already told her. I'm taking some breakfast up to her room; she's rather upset."

Alistair did not usually lose his temper. Years of

controlling his emotions in the classroom had ensued that his personality more often than not stayed on an even keel. As he watched Ann place two bacon rolls on his daughter's One Direction plastic plate with a cup of tea, he felt like punching his wife into the middle of next week.

"I told you *I* wanted to be the one to tell her!" He felt a panic rising in his chest.

"You weren't here, and she needed to know."

"Give me the tray." He snatched it from Ann roughly. "*I'll* take it up."

"Be my guest." Ann's lips hinted at a faint smile. "She won't see you though."

The sound of One Direction could be heard blasting out from his daughter's bedroom as he climbed the stairs carrying the tea and bacon rolls. After knocking at the door and getting no reply, Alistair tried the handle without success.

"Jessie! It's Dad! Can you unlock the door so that I can speak to you?" He knocked again, this time louder, to no avail.

"Jessie; please! It's Dad; open the door!"

"Go away! I don't want to see you anymore!" Jessie's high pitched voice was full of anger. "Go away!"

"Here's some breakfast for you. I love you, Jessie. Don't ever forget that!" He felt tears sting his eyes at the rejection. "Whatever Mum has said, I still love you."

There was no reply. Wounded, hungry and tearful, Alistair put the tray down outside the door, went into his bedroom, took a suitcase out of the wardrobe, and began packing his clothes.

CHAPTER 21

IT WAS STRANGE being in Carly's house on his own; he felt like an intruder. He kept waiting for her to walk in through the front door, but her last text to him had confirmed that she had landed in Detroit and had met up with her sister and brother-in-law. After mentioning the fact that he was now living at her house, he had received a smiley faced emoticon but no other message.

Everything was strange; the cooker, the washing machine, the locks on the back and front doors, and most of all, the silence. No boys' deep voices, no One Direction blasting out from up the stairs, no queues for the bathroom, no meal on the table unless he cooked it himself, and worst of all, plenty of time to think on what he had done to his family. Alistair yearned to see his boys and to hear Jessie's laughter. After a few days of moping about he decided to send a text to Tom.

Hi Tom, how's it going? How's Jessie and Mum? Would love to see you and Jake if you'd like to visit. Love Dad.'

He received a reply almost immediately:

'Hi Dad, we can cycle over tomorrow if you like. How does 2pm grab you? Mum and Jessie are quiet; they don't really say much.'

His heart leapt at the thought of seeing his sons. He quickly composed a reply and sent it.

'2pm is fine. I'm here on my own as Carly is in the States visiting her sister. I'd love for you to meet her when she gets back though.'

He checked in the fridge; the food stores were getting low. He knew the boys would be hungry, and decided that he would have to venture out to build up supplies. He had not done any grocery shopping for a long time, and wondered about quantities and what sort of things to buy. In the end he settled on some pizzas, salad and rolls for the boys, but locating the various items and then queueing at the checkout alongside screaming toddlers and shrieking mothers made him unaccountably irritable. After an execrable wait to pay he realised why Ann would sometimes be harassed on her return from the supermarket.

He was as excited as a child on Christmas Eve as it approached 2pm. He had found the vacuum cleaner, and he was satisfied to see that Carly's thick olive green carpet in the front room now had straight lines up and down it reminiscent of a lawn. He had flicked a duster over the furniture, noticing with approval the uncluttered surfaces free of ornaments and knick-knacks. When the doorbell rang just after 2 o'clock he had to stop himself running to answer it.

"Hey Dude!" Tom's smiling face was beaming.

"Hi Dad!" Jake smiled and craned his neck to see inside the house.

"Hello boys! It's so lovely to see you! Did you find it alright?"

"Yeah; easy peasy." Tom gave a thumbs up.

Leave your bikes round the back; the door's open."

Although it had only been less than a week since he had seen his sons, Alistair was sure they had grown taller in his absence. As they came through the kitchen door he could see Tom was now on eye level with him, and that Jake was only an inch or so shorter.

"Have you two got bigger, or am I shrinking?" He hugged the pair of them and felt like crying again.

"You're shrinking; I'm six feet now." Tom announced proudly. "Although according to my science teacher, my ossification process will soon be complete."

"Smart aleck." Jake gave his brother a kick. "Whatever that is, I'm going to be taller than you anyway."

"In your dreams, cat's meat." Tom stood on tiptoe and looked disdainfully down at Jake.

"Do you two want some pizza and salad?" Alistair smiled, looked from one to the other, and switched on the oven.

"Yeah; we can't wait to taste your cooking." Jake wrinkled his nose. "Mum's knocking us up some roast chicken tonight, but we'll take a chance here."

"How is your mum?" Alistair took some pizzas from the fridge shelf and put them in the oven. "And how is Jessie?"

"All quiet on that front." Tom sprawled on a chair and yawned. "They don't speak to us about anything."

"They jabber on to each other though." Jake nodded. "Mum goes in Jessie's room and shuts the door."

"Does Mum know you've come over here today?" Alistair switched on the oven and turned it up high.

"Er…. no. We told her we were going on a bike ride." Tom smiled.

"Well, we did, didn't we?" Jake looked at Tom as he sat

down next to him.

"Yeah, I suppose so." Tom shrugged.

"Mum knows she still has access to our joint bank account. The mortgage was paid off last year, and so you shouldn't find anything changes where money's concerned." Alistair tried to put the boys' minds at ease. "Hopefully one day she might be able to speak to me, but obviously not yet." He sighed.

"Er….yeah, you're not exactly flavour of the month at the moment." Tom laughed.

"Where's your…er….." Jake appeared embarrassed.

"Carly? She's in the States visiting her sister. Would you like to meet her when she comes back at the end of next week?" Alistair enquired hopefully.

"Sorry, Dad. We'd rather see you on your own at the moment." Tom shook his head.

"That's okay; I understand." Alistair felt a surge of disappointment through his body. "Well, if you two would like to cycle into Attleborough anytime you're free during the school holidays, I'll meet you for lunch somewhere."

"Sure; that'll be great." Tom nodded. "Can I ask a question?"

"Fire away." Alistair sat down with the boys at the kitchen table and wondered what was coming.

"Do you think you and Mum will ever get back together?"

Alistair could see both Tom and Jake were looking at him intently, desperate for an answer. With a sigh he shook his head.

"The way I feel about Carly right now, I can't see it happening. I'm so sorry boys. I never thought anything like this would ever happen to me, but if there's one thing in this life you have to do, you have to be true to yourself. If I lived with Mum now I'd be living a lie, and that's no good for her or for me. It doesn't change how I feel about you two or Jessie, although with Jessie being younger it's going to take her a bit longer to understand."

"We're cool with it all." Tom nodded. "We're blokes, right? I know how it is."

Alistair smiled at his son's perspicacity:

"Thanks for that, son; you always did have an old head on young shoulders."

CHAPTER 22

OUT OF ALL the bleary-eyed passengers who came in on the 06:30 flight from Detroit Metro, Carly was the only one jumping up and down with excitement as she came within sight of him standing expectantly in the Arrivals hall. Alistair's heart started to beat faster at the sight of her red curly head and grin as wide as the Rio Grande.

"Arrrgh!" She ran with her case up to the cordon, jumped over it, and wrapped herself around him.

"Oh, darling it's so good to see you!" He sank his face into her neck and inhaled the scent of her. "I've missed you so much!"

"I'm never going to be apart from you for this long again; ever!" She kissed him passionately, to his eternal embarrassment.

"Not here! Come on; let's get you home."

He grabbed her suitcase with one hand, and Carly's fingers with the other. She bounced along beside him, energised and irrepressible.

"How have you been? Did you work out how to use my

washing machine? Have you washed the sheets yet? Did you see your boys? Any news about Jessie?" Carly squeezed his hand tightly and jumped up to kiss his cheek.

"Steady on! Yes, I've seen the boys; yes I've washed the sheets, but Jessie won't see me." Alistair kissed her forehead. "I'm still hoping on that one."

"She'll come around eventually; give her time." Carly smiled up at him. "I can't wait to get you home and into bed!" She gave a throaty laugh.

"Whatever you're on; I want it." He put his arm around her shoulders and chuckled. "Are you on uppers or something?"

"No, just in love." She put her head on his shoulder briefly. "And pleased to see her man."

The short-term car park was empty of people. Alistair extricated himself from Carly's grasp, opened the boot of the car, and stowed away the luggage. As he closed the boot he saw a tell-tale gleam in her eye.

"Come and sit on the back seat; there's nobody about. I want to show you how much I love you." She winked at him and opened one of the back doors.

Alistair, to his surprise, found himself with an unexpected erection as he sat down, closed the door, and looked worriedly from side to side out of the windows:

"There's nobody about." Carly laughed and kneeled over him. "Let's unzip your trousers."

"Carly…."

Somehow the real chance that they could be caught caused an unusual feeling of excitement to shoot through him. As she freed his penis and straddled him, his breathing increased and he ran a hand underneath her skirt.

"You're not wearing any underwear." He whispered, and cupped her buttocks with his hands.

"No shit, Sherlock!"

She lowered herself down onto him, and just for a few moments of ecstasy he let himself drown in her body, obliterating everything except the feel of her and his own sudden desire for release.

"See? There's still nobody about. We could do it all over again." Carly, sitting demurely in the front seat, crossed her legs and laughed.

"Give over; we've probably been caught on a security camera somewhere." He looked up out of the windscreen and started the engine. "I can see one on the other side over there."

"Oh well, they've probably had a little thrill if they've been watching." Carly stuck up her middle finger in the air as the car moved slowly past the camera. "I was just happy to see you!"

"You can be pleased to see me any time." Alistair smiled as waited for the barrier to rise. "But I'd be even more pleased in the comfort of our bed."

"Yeah; well. Sometimes you just have to live dangerously." She yawned. "I'm going to sleep now; wake me up when we get home."

Home.

He was still unused to the fact that 'home' meant Carly's terraced house on the outskirts of Attleborough. As he drove back up the M11 he thought back to all the years he had struggled to pay the mortgage on the semi-detached property he had bought a few years into his marriage. When he had completed the last payment and received the deeds he and Ann had gone out celebrating. Now he would have to start paying his share of Carly's mortgage as well as paying the bills on the house he had struggled so long to own but would now never possess.

He looked across at the woman he loved so passionately, sleeping silently on the front seat, and hoped against hope all the upheaval he had caused would be worth it in the long run.

CHAPTER 23

HE WOULD ALWAYS look back fondly on the rest of those idyllic summer holidays with her. The memories of quietly waking up next to Carly; eating breakfast and making love in the now-familiar black bedroom before hiking in the countryside or driving up to the North Norfolk coast for the remainder of the day would stay etched in his mind forever.

As he woke up one Monday morning in early September with the sun streaming in through the curtains, Alistair stretched out happily in bed, thought of the new term looming, and considered himself very fortunate indeed at being able to live and work with the woman he adored. He glanced over at Carly, still asleep next to him, and decided to creep downstairs and cook up a feast for their breakfast.

He edged out of bed, hardly making any movement to disturb the sleeper, threw on a towelling robe, and slipped his feet into the furry moccasins Carly had bought for him which he disliked intensely but had not had the heart to tell her. As he yawned and padded down the stairs he was surprised to hear the doorbell ring. Tying his robe tighter, he smoothed back his hair and unlocked the front door, instantly alert and more than a little worried to see two policemen standing there.

"Alistair Anthony Veale?"

"Yes." Alistair looked from one to the other in puzzlement.

"May we come in?" The taller of the two had already set foot across the threshold.

"What's happened? Has something happened to my wife or children?" Alistair opened the door fully to allow them access.

"Mr Veale; I am Detective Sergeant David Broughton-Ives of the Norfolk Constabulary's Child Abuse Investigation Unit. This is PC Williams. There has been a serious allegation made against you and you are under arrest. I'm afraid you will need to get dressed and come with us down to the station for questioning."

Alistair felt like laughing at the absurdity of it. Upstairs he could hear the floorboards creak as Carly got out of bed:

"Who's there, Ali?" He heard her voice at the top of the stairs.

"It's the police." Alistair wondered if he was in some sort of dream. "Apparently I'm under arrest and need to go down to the station for questioning."

"Why?" Carly came quickly down the stairs, tying a dressing gown around her middle.

"That's what I want to know." Alistair looked blankly at the two officers.

"Mr Veale, there has been an allegation of child sexual abuse made against you. Information has been passed to us from the NSPCC. Due to the seriousness with which we treat these cases, we are arresting you forthwith. You do not have to say anything, but it may harm your defence if you do not mention when questioned something which you later rely on in court. Anything you do say may be given in evidence. We have a warrant to search the premises. We will be taking away your computer and mobile phone for inspection. Please get dressed and come with us."

Alistair stood open-mouthed for what seemed like an eternity, looking at the officers' grim faces and then back to an equally incredulous Carly.

"This is madness! I haven't done anything! It's not my computer, it's my partner's!" He shook his head. "Who's made the accusation?"

"We have information passed to us that the accuser is your daughter, Jessica Ann Veale." Detective Sergeant Broughton-Ives looked around him. "You have until the time we have gathered evidence here to eat, drink, wash, and get dressed."

"What? He hasn't seen her for weeks! What's she playing at?" Carly shook her head. "Ali, I'm coming with you."

"No need; I'll be home in no time. This is all a terrible mistake." Alistair looked at the officers. "We've just got out of bed; I'd like a shower and a coffee if you don't mind."

"I'll make it; you run and get ready." Carly went into the kitchen and switched on the kettle.

While the police officers searched for evidence, Alistair completed the quickest shower and shave of his life, snatched a quick coffee, dressed hastily in clothes from the previous day, and then followed the men out of the door. His stomach was turning cartwheels, and he was glad he had not eaten anything. The ride to the station was taken in silence, and on stepping out of the car one officer walked on either side of him up to the station desk, making him feel like a hardened criminal.

"Mr Veale, we're going to take all your details and fingerprints. You will then be taken to an interview room." DS Broughton-Ives nodded to the Duty Sergeant.

"I want a solicitor present. This is a false accusation. I need a solicitor to be in the interview room with me who is experienced in this sort of thing." Alistair hoped his stomach would hold onto the cup of coffee; his heart was racing as though he had just run a marathon.

"Very well; you will be held here in custody until Aiden Lumley arrives. He's the solicitor we use in these types of cases." DS Broughton-Ives replied politely.

"I assume his fees will be paid for under Legal Aid?" Alistair, aghast at the possible expense, looked at the Detective Sergeant.

"Yes, that's correct. I'll phone Mr Lumley's secretary now. Constable Williams will take your details and fingerprints while I phone the secretary."

DS Broughton-Ives indicated to PC Williams to take over, and after stating his name, address and date of birth, Alistair found himself in the unenviable position of being fingerprinted like a common criminal, all the time still wondering if he was in some sort of nightmare. Satisfied at having given any information as truthfully and courteously as he could, Alistair followed the constable to a sparsely furnished interview room, pleased to be able to sit down at last and gather his thoughts in peace. However, the minutes soon turned into hours as he waited for the solicitor, and he marked off the time passing by meals brought to him via the custody officer; overcooked bacon, eggs and toast on his arrival, and ham salad sandwiches and cake when his stomach began growling with hunger again. He breathed a sigh of relief when eventually a pin-stripe suited, well-groomed man in his mid-fifties appeared carrying a briefcase and accompanied by DS Broughton-Ives."

"Mr Veale, this is Aiden Lumley, your solicitor. We are going to record the interview, and Mr Lumley will be taking notes. You will only receive a transcript of the recording if you are charged."

Alistair nodded briefly to the solicitor, unsure of what was coming next. As he sat up alert in his chair, he felt that in fact he could state with absolute certainty that after the morning's activities, he would never be quite so sure about anything ever again.

CHAPTER 24

"INTERVIEW WITH Mr Alistair Anthony Veale; three fifteen pm on Monday September first, two thousand and fourteen. Present is Alistair Veale, Aiden Lumley, Solicitor, PC Kevin Williams, and myself, DS David Broughton-Ives." DS Broughton-Ives spoke into the microphone of the voice recorder before placing it down on the table and looking at Alistair.

"Can you confirm your name and address, please?"

DS Broughton-Ives' manner was amiable, and Alistair relaxed slightly:

"Alistair Anthony Veale, eighty five Juniper Mews, Attleborough, Norfolk, although this is my partner, Carly Jessop's house. I had previously been living at five Greengage Close, Buckingham, Norfolk, for eighteen years prior to living at Juniper Mews."

"Do you own the property at five Greengage Close?"

"Yes; my wife and children live there."

"But now you're not residing at the family home?"

"No; I'm separated from my wife."

"How long have you been living at Juniper Mews?" "Oh; only since the end of July when my wife and I separated."

"Because of your infidelity with Miss Jessop." "Correct."

"How old are you? What is your date of birth?" DS Broughton-Ives sat back in his chair and looked at Alistair.

"I'm forty two. I was born on eighth December nineteen seventy one."

"And what do you do for a living?"

"I'm head of the English department at Oakleigh Academy, Attleborough."

"Due to the nature of these allegations, we will need to inform the head teacher at the academy. Who is that please?"

"Mr Leonard Carter." Alistair felt a terrible sinking sensation in the pit of his stomach. "Am I going to lose my job over this insanity? I've worked there for fifteen years and have a totally clean record! I've just taken fourteen kids to the Isle of Wight for God's sake! Each one of them can testify that I'm not a pervert!"

"Do your children attend the school where you teach?" DS Broughton-Ives took a notebook out of his pocket.

"No; my wife and I thought it best from the start that they did not."

"Mr Veale, if you are charged we will bring witnesses to court to testify for your good character." Aiden Lumley nodded. "It's best that you just answer the questions that are put to you at the moment."

Alistair nodded, suddenly distraught at the implications of his daughter's actions.

"Mr Veale, we have had a phone call from the NSPCC asking us to investigate your daughter's allegations." DS

Broughton-Ives sat forward again and leafed through his notebook.

"Which are?" Alistair looked the detective sergeant straight in the eyes.

"That you have repeatedly forced her to commit sexual acts over a period of the last five years."

"This is absolute insanity." Alistair shook his head. "We had a normal, loving father/daughter relationship until I left her mother and moved in with Miss Jessop. Her mother's poisoned Jessie against me. I never had a chance to explain the separation to her."

"Have you ever touched your daughter inappropriately, asked her to perform sexual acts with you, or had sexual intercourse with her?"

Alistair kept the detective sergeant's gaze, his heart hammering ferociously in his chest:

"No; absolutely not. Never!" He shook his head again. "If you don't believe me, get Jessie examined! Surely a doctor can testify that she's a virgin?"

"Yes, the medical officer will examine your daughter." DS Broughton-Ives sighed. "But she is accusing you of sexual acts not associated with vaginal intercourse."

"Such as what?" Alistair, incredulous, ran a hand through his hair and over his face in weariness.

"Fellatio."

"Jessie wouldn't know anything at all about that! She's only thirteen and has been very sheltered! My wife would have put her up to it out of revenge."

"Let's talk about your relationship with your wife and with Miss Jessop. Do you have sexual relations with Miss Jessop, your current partner?"

"Yes; we have a normal healthy sex life." Alistair nodded.

"What about Ann Veale, your wife?"

"Our sex life was dying; our marriage was just coasting along. When I met Carly I fell in love. It's as simple as that."

"When you had a sex life with your wife, what was it like?"

"Unfulfilling, for me anyway; also not very often. I've a feeling Ann did not really like sex at all."

"But you do."

"Yes."

"What kind of sex do you like?"

"Is this relevant?" Alistair looked at Aiden Lumley. "Do I have to answer this?"

"No; you have a perfect right to decline to answer the question." Aiden Lumley scribbled on a notepad.

"I don't want to answer that one." Alistair could feel tears stinging his eyes and looked down at the table until the sensation passed.

"Where does Miss Jessop work?" DS Broughton-Ives jotted down a few notes.

"At the Oakleigh Academy with me. She's a Science teacher."

"I see. And when did the professional relationship take a more personal turn?"

"She came with me on a school trip to the Isle of Wight in July to look after the six girls. I had eight boys to keep an eye on. We just clicked; I had no inkling anything like that was going to happen."

"You'd not had any feelings for her before the trip?"

"No; she was new at her post. I'd noticed her in the staff room, but nothing had happened before the trip. Can I have a cup of tea please? I'm really thirsty." Alistair sighed. "When will I be able to go home?"

"Okay; PC Williams will fetch us some." DS Broughton-Ives signalled to the constable. "Mr Veale, we will decide today whether to charge you with gross indecency with a minor and keep you in custody until your court case, or release you on bail while investigations into the alleged offences are carried out. Investigations will take some time because we will need to check your phone and any computers you have used at your wife's address, your new address, and at the school where you teach. Our medical officer will also need to examine your daughter and take her statement."

"I'm innocent; I would never, ever, think of having sex with my own daughter or anybody underage. My livelihood depends on that." Alistair closed his eyes in grief. "Oh God; term starts next Monday! Am I going to be able to work while all these inquiries are carried out?"

"That's for the head teacher to decide. My guess is that you'll be suspended though; it's the usual procedure."

"This is an absolute nightmare." Alistair placed his head in his hands. "I just can't believe it! I need to contact the Union, the NASUWT; this is so wrong. What happens about pay? If I'm suspended, will I be paid? My family rely on my wages."

"It is usual in these matters to receive normal salary pending the results of the inquiries." Aiden Lumley nodded at a relieved Alistair from his seat opposite.

The door to the interview room opened and Alistair looked up to see PC Williams carrying a tray laden with cups and a teapot.

"Tea and biscuits Mr Veale." PC Williams laid the tray down in the middle of the table.

"Thanks." Alistair sighed. "Thanks very much."

He had suffered the indignity of being escorted to the toilet; now Alistair sat in the interview room awaiting his fate. Tired but unable to relax, he felt permanently on edge and terrified regarding his future. After DS Broughton-Ives had returned to the interview room and the custody officer had left, the detective sergeant took a seat opposite Alistair.

"Mr Veale, I have had a word with the Chief Superintendent. We are going to release you on bail, under condition that you sign in every week here at the station, and do not attempt to contact any members of your family or visit the family home during the course of the inquiries. Please do not travel abroad until the investigation is complete, which may take several weeks. When it is complete, a file will be sent to the Crown Prosecution Service, who will decide whether or not there is sufficient evidence to place the matter before a court. We will contact your employer, who will no doubt call you to arrange a meeting. We will see you next Saturday morning at nine o'clock for your first signing on, but on a lighter note, when you have signed your custody record you will be free to go. You may use the telephone at the front desk to call your partner so that she can come and collect you." The detective sergeant stood up and walked towards the door. "I will ask the custody officer to come back in. Read the record carefully and note anything which needs correcting."

There was a brief moment when the room emptied of people. Alistair closed his eyes and exhaled slowly, stunned and traumatised beyond belief.

CHAPTER 25

"ALI, YOU'VE GOT to talk to Ann; this thing is madness."

Alistair, slumped uncomfortably into the passenger seat of Carly's Micra, looked at the outside of the police station and heaved a sigh of relief as it disappeared from view.

"I'm not allowed to talk to anyone from the family as part of my bail conditions." He cleared his throat, trying to rid his voice of its shakiness.

"Yeah, but surely this is an exception? Ann knows full well that Jessie's lying." Carly joined the flow of traffic heading towards the outskirts of Attleborough. "You can't let them get away with this."

"Of course she knows it's all a lie; she put Jessie up to it. I daren't risk calling her though; would you, if you were in my shoes?"

"I'd go round there and bloody well beat the crap out of her."

"Oh yeah, I can just see that helping my case no end." He gave a rueful laugh. "It's just revenge; pure and simple, and at the moment it must be giving them both a great deal of satisfaction, especially now I can't speak to the boys either."

Picking up speed as they left the main town centre, Alistair enjoyed the views of the open countryside and relaxed slightly as the road emptied of traffic. He put a hand on Carly's knee and gave it a squeeze.

"This is so much better than sitting in that interview room. Thanks for picking me up today and believing in me. I'd never touch a hair on Jessie's head; you know that, don't you?"

"Of course." She briefly rested her hand on top of his. "I'll put in a good word for you with Leonard. Do you want me to explain our situation to him?"

"I suppose it might be best under the circumstances, but I didn't really want us to be the talk of the staff room."

"We'll ask him to keep it confidential. I'll come with you when you're called in; it's bound to be this week before term starts." She raised his hand and gave it a kiss. "Don't worry."

"I'm fucking petrified." He felt stubborn tears return. "If I lose my job I'm buggered; I'll never be able to find another one; my card will be marked. Whatever the outcome is, it'll be on my record forever now." He wiped his eyes. "Shit; how could they do this to me?"

He was aware that the car had come to a halt. When he looked up he saw Carly had parked haphazardly in a lay-by:

"Don't cry, darling; come here." She leaned over and put her arms around him. "I love you; we'll work through this together."

"I love you, Carly." He sank his head into her shoulder and sobbed. "I'm so sorry for all of this."

"It's not your fault. If you do lose your job then Ann will find she suddenly has no income. If I were you, in the meantime I'd move any funds to another account where she can't get at it. In that way she'll have to contact you to ask for money, and you'll then be able to read her the riot act. If she can play dirty, then so will we. What do you say? Shall we go back to town and visit the bank?" She kissed his head gently.

"Yes; do it." He sniffed. "My reputation is fucked now, thanks to her. She's not having my money as well, that'll really be taking the piss; I'll draw as much of it out as I can. It's too late to open up another account today; the bank will be closed. We'll go back in the morning and speak to somebody at the other bank opposite. When she finds out there's no money left she'll have to speak to me or sign on at the benefits office; I'd love to be a fly on the wall when she realises that. Although, on the other hand, they'll probably give her more money than she'll ever get from me anyway. This country's way too soft."

"Yeah, but at least she'll have to grovel for it; two can play at that game." Carly swung the car around. "Dry your eyes Mister; this is war."

He stood numbly in the High Street with his arm around Carly's shoulder, waiting for the queue to reduce at the cash machine. All around him people were going about their daily business, laughing, chatting, and hurrying home from work. He felt jealous of their happiness, more stressed than he had ever felt in his entire life, and bone-achingly tired. As he moved to the head of the queue he fished in his wallet for his bank card.

"I was paid last Friday; there should be about three thousand pounds in there." He inserted the card in the slot and put in his pin number. "I'll try and take out five hundred and see what happens." He pressed the button for a balance. "Shit!"

"What? What's the matter?" Carly peered at the display screen.

"She's taken it! There's fuck all in there!" He punched the wall above the machine, not caring if anybody behind him was listening. "There's nothing left!" He punched the wall again, grazing his knuckles and then leaning his forehead on the cold steel of the machine. "Fuck it; fuck them all!" He pressed the button to retrieve his card and turned away, brushing unseeingly past the startled person behind him.

"Don't worry; she can't get at *my* wages; I'll keep us both until you get paid again." Carly ran to keep up with him. "You've got time to set up another account before the end of the month. It'll take a few weeks before she can get the Child Support people involved."

"Yeah; I'll have to pay when they contact me, but tonight I'm going to write letters to the utility companies and tell them I don't live there anymore." Alistair kicked a stone furiously as he strode along. "She can pay her own fucking bills out of her dole money; she's left nothing in there to cover the standing orders."

"Good for you!" Carly slipped a hand in his. "I'll help you any way I can. I'll even do some of the letters for you. Let's get home and get cracking straight away, but slow down; I can't keep up!" She ran alongside him, breathless.

"Sorry; I'm just furious." He slowed his pace. "I never thought she would react like this."

"Well she has, and we've got to deal with it. All you did is fall in love with me. It's not a crime, and I'm going to make bloody sure that you're not treated like a criminal. I'm with you all the way on this."

"Thanks, baby." He sighed and gave her hand a squeeze as they approached the car. "I love you so much."

CHAPTER 26

HE KNEW THE meeting would have to take place eventually, but just two days after Ann's revelations he sat facing the head of the academy alongside Carly and representatives from the union and governing body. Leonard Carter, seemingly embarrassed, took off his reading glasses, shuffled papers, and gave Alistair a wan smile.

"I've called this meeting because as you know, I've had a call from the police regarding yourself and the allegations of sexual abuse by your daughter."

"Yes." Alistair nodded. "Leonard, I have to tell you straight off; Carly is my partner now, that's why she's here, and Jessie's allegations have been made out of spite, aided by my wife I'm sure. There's no truth to any of them."

"I've known you for many years." Leonard nodded. "And I must say the accusation has completely taken me by surprise. However, I must adhere to the correct procedures as required by the police and the school's governing body."

"Leonard; I'm speaking for Ali as well." Carly leaned forward in her chair. "His relationship with his daughter was fine until he fell in love with me. I can vouch that I'm the reason this unfortunate episode has come about."

"Thank you, Carly." Leonard cleared his throat. "However, Alistair, I must suspend you while the investigations are carried out. I shall announce that you're taking special leave for personal reasons at the first assembly next week and also in the school's newsletter, but of course you shall still receive full pay. I have to tell you that you will not be allowed on school premises or be able to speak to any pupils until the suspension has been lifted by the governing body. I also do not need to tell you or Carly about strict confidentiality regarding this issue."

"Thanks Leonard; of course we'll keep it confidential, as we hope you'll do the same." Alistair nodded. "I need to give you some new bank account details for my wages."

"That's fine; you can contact me if you have any questions or wish to be kept updated with developments at school or with the investigation. I will put what I've said to you today in writing and will post it to you." Leonard looked kindly at Alistair. "Where are you living now?"

"With Carly; you can mail anything to her address." Alistair took hold of Carly's hand.

"If you would like some stress counselling I can give you somebody to contact?" Leonard enquired.

"No, I'm okay. "Alistair shook his head. "It was a bit of a shock to start with, but I'm coming to terms with it now. I just can't believe Ann would do something like this." He took a piece of paper out of his wallet. "Here's the new bank account; I've had to change it because she's cleaned me out totally. There's nothing left in there at all."

"I must say this all seems completely out of character for both of you." Leonard agreed. "I've seen Ann on many occasions, and I have to say I'm completely flabbergasted by the allegations."

"Me too. I'm still reeling from the shock." Alistair nodded at Leonard and the reps as he stood up. "Keep me updated; I look forward to hearing from you." He shook Leonard's hand.

"All the best Ali; hope to meet with you soon." Leonard grasped Alistair's hand. "See you on Monday, Carly."

"Come to bed; I'll make it all go away for an hour or two." Carly unlocked the front door and turned to Alistair.

"I can't even raise a smile at the moment, let alone anything else." Alistair sighed and walked down the hallway to the kitchen. "If only we were back on the Isle of Wight again."

"If you had known what was going to happen then, would you still have had sex with me?" Carly followed him into the kitchen and switched on the kettle.

"Oh yes. I love you; nothing's going to change that." He kissed her forehead. "It's all over with Ann."

"I feel guilty, breaking up your home though." She took some milk out of the fridge.

"Don't; I *want* to be here with you." He nodded.

"I hope she's regretting what she's done." Carly added some coffee to two mugs and chuckled. "Anyway, she will when it's payday again."

"I hate to think of my kids going without." Alistair sat down at the table.

"They won't." Carly shook her head. "She'll soon be claiming benefits. But hey, you have to live too, *and* you don't know if you're going to lose your job."

"I feel like a parasite, living off you."

"It's only for this month; you can chuck at me any amount of money you like after payday." Carly laughed held her hand out. "Come on; fivers, tenners, fifties; *give me the money!*"

"I'll pay the mortgage; it'll make me feel better."

"We can discuss it when you find out how much the Child Support people want."

"The majority of it, probably; after they're finished with me I'll have fuck all." Alistair put his hands behind his head and stretched. "Ann will go ballistic next payday, and of course, it's all going to be my fault."

"You'll always have me on your side, if that's any consolation?" Carly poured some boiling water into the mugs and added some milk. "When I saw you get out of the minibus on that Sunday morning in the school car park, I fancied you straight away."

"Did you?" He took the mug from her and smiled. "Thanks; by the way, I had a hard-on as soon as I saw you sitting on your rucksack." He took a few sips of coffee and gazed at her.

"Dirty devil! See.... You can smile after all!" She caressed the front of his trousers. "Come upstairs; I want to make your smile a bit bigger."

"Okay, but just lie on top of me; I want to hold you."

Once again she had been right; the sex *had* made him forget about everything. He lay with his eyes closed and enjoyed the feel of Carly's naked body on top of his.

"Your skin is so soft." He caressed her back and ran his fingers through her hair. "You're amazing."

"I bet you say that to all the girls." She propped herself up on his chest with her elbows and smiled at him.

"There's only been Ann, also Maggie who I told you about, and a couple of girls before my marriage; I can't even remember their names or what they looked like." He repressed the urge to ask her about the number of men she had slept with.

"I'm so glad we're together." Carly grinned at him.

"I need to ask you one question, though." He teased out a red curl and wrapped it around his finger.

"What?"

"Won't you want any children? I mean……"

"Because my body clock's ticking away?" She kissed him. "No; I teach kids but I don't want any of my own, thanks very much."

"Well that's okay then, 'cos remember I've had my firing pin removed."

"It seems to be working okay to me." She laughed. "Not *that*; you know what I mean…." He yawned. "I'm sleepy in the middle of the day."

"That's because I've worn you out, you poor old man."

"I'm going to be productive over the next few weeks though; I'm not going to sit around on my arse and do nothing while you're at work." He opened his eyes and looked at her. "Leonard's given me gardening leave, so I'm going to dig your garden."

"You can dig my garden any time." Carly guffawed.

"God! Your dirty little mind!" He laughed. "I'll make myself useful around the house. Give me a list of jobs that need doing and I'll do them."

"I've got a list as long as your winkle."

"Oh, not very many then?" He wrapped his arms

around her and squeezed. "I'll have to concentrate on your garden."

"Sounds good to me."

CHAPTER 27

HE HAD ALWAYS needed a reason to get up in the mornings. For as long as he could remember he had thankfully had one; to drive off each morning to the teaching job that he loved, which put food on the table for his family and made him feel productive and needed. However, with Carly back at work and all the outstanding jobs completed around the house, Alistair was finding the days had started to drag. As September turned into October he was reduced to digging over flowerbeds and trimming the hedges and trees in Carly's quite substantial garden. One balmy morning as he cut back a particularly rampant pampas on the front lawn, he was quite unaware of being watched until a familiar voice broke through his reverie.

"Hello Alistair."

Hot and sweaty, he looked up and received a sudden shock from the person standing at the garden gate:

"Ann; what are you doing here?" He rubbed the dirt off his hands and stood looking at his wife.

"Tom gave me your address. I need to speak to you."

"I'm not supposed to contact anyone from the family as

part of my bail conditions." Alistair shrugged.

"Well, I've come to see *you*, so it doesn't matter. Can I come in for a moment?" She looked beyond him. "Is she......"

"Carly's at work. What do you want?"

"Shall we talk out here then, or do you want all the neighbours listening? Ann rested one hand on the gate.

"Come in then." He sighed. "I'll just go and wash my hands."

He decided not to offer her a drink. After cleaning up at the sink he came into the front room where she sat stiff and cross-legged on the settee. He sat himself down in an armchair opposite and waited for the inevitable request.

"The bank account's empty."   Ann looked directly at him.

"I know; you cleaned me out." He met her gaze, unsmiling.

"I'm sorry about that; I was angry." She reddened and looked away.

"So was I when you did it. Guess what I did? I opened up another account for my wages to go in, so that you can't do it again." He looked at her triumphantly.

"I need money for the children; you must have been paid again by now." She bit a nail and sighed.

"Get a job, then." He suddenly hated the sight of her for what she had done to him.

"Are you refusing to support your children?"

"No; but you'll have to go through the CSA. I'm sure they'll let me know how much I have to pay."

"You bastard!" She stood up. "You walk out of our marriage and now you're leaving us without a penny!"

"You seem to have forgotten why I've suddenly become less than accommodating." He stood up and faced her. "In case you need reminding I'm suspended from work because Jessie's accused me of being a paedophile! I've been interviewed by the police, am out on bail, and my reputation is ruined! I may never work again! If you're short of money now, just think how you'll be when I'm on the dole permanently or banged up! I suppose all this didn't have anything to do with you, did it?" His breathing came ragged with anger.

"Jessie did it off her own bat." Ann looked down at the carpet.

"Oh yeah, pull the other one!" He took a step towards her. "You know I worshipped the ground she walked on." His voice cracked. "She's unworldly; how would she know about oral sex? How could you do that? It's wicked!"

"She….she was devastated that you'd left her."   Ann sat down again. "She cried herself to sleep night after night. You weren't there. I was angry you'd done that to her; she's at a very vulnerable age."

"So you filled her head with knowledge that thirteen year olds shouldn't know about and gave her the number of the NSPCC, and you say I'm wicked?" He laughed. "My God, Ann; that takes the biscuit, it really does!" He flopped down, spent, into the armchair.

"I never told her anything about oral sex; she already knew. Kids talk in the playground. It was never meant to go as far as it did; she took it upon herself to say those things. Look; I've had time to cool down now. If you like we can come to some sort of arrangement." She crossed her legs again and composed herself. "I'll get Jessie to drop the charges, just as long as you pay some money into the joint account."

"Mud sticks even if charges *are* dropped; I'll never be able to hold my head up in that school again! I can't even see or speak to my sons! You should have thought all this out properly before you hatched your little plan with our daughter." He waggled a finger at her. "You've fucked up my life! Do you realise that, you stupid woman?"

"I'm sorry, Ali." Ann began to cry. "As I said, it was never meant to go as far as it did. Jessie was only supposed to phone the NSPCC and complain that you wouldn't give her any privacy or let her go out with a boyfriend, or something like that. I wanted you to suffer; I was so angry that I'd been cast out like some worn out shoe."

"And I *am* suffering! You've got what you wanted! I was prepared to pay all the bills and give you money for anything you needed. I had no intention of leaving you destitute, but you can't do what you did to me and expect me to happily hand over my money. It's not going to happen." He shook his head, unmoved by her tears. "If this all goes to court any barrister will tear Jessie apart in the witness box. You don't stand a flying fuck of winning this. Has she been examined?"

"Examined? By whom?" Ann looked at him, perplexed.

"By the police doctor. It'll have to be confirmed that she's still a virgin."

"Oh, God! Surely not!" Ann put a hand to her mouth.

"I'm afraid she *will* be examined if it goes to court, because the results will be needed by the barrister for my defence." Alistair looked grim. "You really didn't think this out very well, did you?"

"I'll have a word with her. I'll get her to drop the charges straight away." Ann wiped her eyes. "She went way over my head with this; it all got out of hand and snowballed too fast. She must have phoned them again when I wasn't listening. She's angry, Ali, as angry as I am, but she didn't realise the trouble you'd get into. She's just a kid."

"Yeah, well maybe you can tell her what's been going on here; she might end up visiting me in jail if she carries on with this."

"I'll go now and speak to her when she comes out of school. If she drops the charges, will you pay some money into the joint account?" Ann sniffed, picked up her bag and stood up.

"I'd need confirmation from the police and Leonard first that I'm exonerated and that my life can get back to normal." "It will; I'll speak to her. Goodbye for now. I'll see myself out." Ann walked towards the door.

"'Bye."

He remained seated, shocked at what he had heard, but now holding out the faint hope that there could possibly be some light at the end of a long, dark tunnel.

CHAPTER 28

"YOU'RE GETTING BETTER at cooking." Carly sniffed appreciably as she came into the kitchen. "What's for dinner tonight?"

"Roast pork for a change; glad I can be useful." Alistair smiled. "How's school?" He kissed her, enjoying the contact after a day alone.

"It seems I've been passed over for promotion. I didn't get Head of Science after all." She put her arms around his neck and sighed.

"Try again next year; the investigation might have something to do with it?" Alistair gave her a squeeze. "Has anybody spoken to you about me?"

"No; nobody. It's either an open secret or Leonard's kept it to himself; I'm not sure which yet." She shrugged and sat down.

"Let's hope the latter; I had a little visitor today." He glanced at her as he began to stir some gravy.

"Oh? Who?" She looked up at him with interest.

"Ann."

"Surprise, surprise. The money must have run out." Carly chuckled.

"It has."

"What did you tell her?"

"To get a job and contact the CSA."

"Ha! Good for you!" She laughed.

"She admitted that everything had got out of hand. Apparently it wasn't meant to go this far. Ann and Jessie had been angry, but Jess was only supposed to complain about me not giving her any privacy or something minor just to get her own back."

"So what went wrong then?"

"She carried on being angry that I'd gone, talked to other girls at school I expect, and spouted off again to the NSPCC without Ann's knowledge, but didn't realise the shit that she'd cause."

"So Ann's confirmed it was a hoax call?"

"Yeah." He turned the heat off under the gravy and cut the pork joint into slices.

"Jeez; you should have recorded the conversation and played it back to the police."

"Ann's going to speak to Jessie. She knows that no money will be in the joint account unless all the charges are dropped. With a bit of luck it looks like everything's going to work out now." He took out two warm plates from under the grill. "Shall we open a bottle of wine to celebrate?"

"I'll get one." Carly stood up. "Congratulations, Mr Veale. Hopefully I'll be able to lust after you in the staff room soon." She put her arms around his waist.

"You can lust after me now if you like." Alistair kissed her open mouth. "I don't mind."

"After dinner; your gravy's getting cold."

He sat by the phone, willing it to ring. When no call materialised he was sorely tempted to contact Ann to find out what was going on, but still mindful of the bail conditions, decided to wait a while longer. Answering the doorbell three days after the conversation with his wife, he was surprised to receive a second visit:

"Hi." He kept his expression neutral.

"Hello Ali; I won't stay long, but I need to speak to you."

"You'd better come in then."

As Ann walked haughtily past him into the hallway he resisted the urge to grab her by the throat. He closed the door and turned to face her.

"Go through to the front room. Would you like a drink?"

"No thanks; what I have to say won't take long."

He chose the same armchair again so as not to sit too near to her. He watched her as she sat primly down on the settee and crossed her legs.

"What's going on?" He tapped his fingers on the arm of the chair impatiently.

"Jessie's not going to retract her accusation. She says you did molest her and that it went on for some time. She was too scared to say anything when you were still living at home."

His heart thumped painfully in his chest as he watched her mouth forming the words, seemingly in slow motion; all hopes of redemption dashed:

"This is lunacy! You *know* she's doing this out of revenge!" He thumped the armchair with his fist. "You admitted before that you put her up to it!"

"Yes I know. She says she was frightened and wasn't aware who to phone about it before, but when I gave her the NSPCC's number she waited until I was in the garden and couldn't hear, and then phoned them again in secret. Have you abused her, Ali?"

He saw his wife's eyes fill with tears and looked away. In the past he would have rushed to comfort her, but this time he needed to stand his ground and remain focused; his livelihood depended on it.

"I can't believe you would even ask me such a question!" He shook his head vigorously. "All I've done is fall in love with another woman. I know it's hit Jessie hard that I'm not living at home anymore, but you've got to make her see reason! I can't even begin to think why you told her to ring the NSPCC in the first place!" Alistair exhaled forcefully. "I realise you wanted revenge, but this is going to affect us all if I'm sent to jail!" He closed his eyes at the thought of it.

"Why did you always insist on bathing her and putting her to bed? You were always up there for ages in her room every evening with the door shut. One night I came up and tried the door; it was locked. I know our sex life was not up to much, but I found it strange that you never seemed to mind. I often used to wonder if you were getting your jollies elsewhere." Ann's voice wobbled with emotion and she wiped her eyes.

"All I used to do was read her a few stories for God's sake! If the door was locked then Jessie must have done it to stop the boys coming in and teasing her." He sighed. "I'd been at work all day; it was my time with my daughter. I wanted to forge a bond while she was still young. If I'd been abusing her night after night she wouldn't have wanted me in there, surely?" He threw up his hands in supplication. "Come on; we've been married for twenty years! Am I a monster or not? Answer me!" His eyes bored into hers.

"No; you're not a monster, but I need to know why she's behaving like this."

"Because she's pissed off that her old man has gone! That's why!" He counted to ten mentally. "Look; to show you I'm not Jack the fucking Ripper reincarnated I'll even put some money in the joint account for you."

"Thank you. Oh, and by the way, the medical officer phoned yesterday; he wants to examine Jessie."

"Fine; I'm sure he'll find she's still a virgin." He nodded. "If she isn't, then it's got nothing to do with me. It's best that you don't come round here anymore, if somebody sees you here I'll be in even more trouble."

"Very well then, I'll wait to find out the result of the examination and we'll take it from there." She stood up. "Goodbye, Ali; I'll see myself out."

"'Bye."

As the front door closed he sank back in the chair and closed his eyes.

CHAPTER 29

HE HATED SIGNING in at the police station; the whole process was humiliating and made him feel just like the criminal they imagined him to be. As he announced himself to the desk sergeant one Saturday morning in mid-October, the now familiar figure of DS Broughton-Ives materialised from somewhere behind the front desk:

"Mr Veale; when you've signed in please could you step into my office."

"With a dry mouth and clammy palms, Alistair wrote his signature somewhat shakily on the form that had been pushed in front of him. The desk sergeant scrutinised him as he led him through a side entrance.

"Second door on the right."

"Thanks."

The detective sergeant sat leafing through some paperwork behind a large ancient-looking desk.

"Mr Veale; come in. I thought I'd let you know the result of our investigations so far." He put the papers down on the desk and indicated towards a chair opposite. "Take a seat. How have you been getting on?"

"Okay, I suppose. I've been making myself useful around the house; gardening and doing odd jobs. I like to keep busy." Alistair nodded.

"Well, I can tell you that your computers and phone have been examined now, and the medical officer has compiled his report on your daughter."

Alistair's heart began to race, and he mentally crossed his fingers and toes:

"Anything to find?" His voice came out strangled with fear.

"Nothing at all on either computer or on your phone. Your daughter's hymen is intact, and there are no signs of sexual abuse."

"Thanks for letting me know." He let out a sigh of relief. "What happens now?"

"We will pass our findings to Mr Carter and the school governing body, who will convene and decide whether to take matters further or lift the suspension."

"So I'm still suspended, even though there's nothing to find?" Alistair was pleased to discover his voice sounded more confident now. "Can I have my phone back please? My partner would also like to have her computer returned."

"We will have to wait until we're informed by the governing body of their decision." DS Broughton-Ives smiled. "But rest assured we have found nothing untoward."

As he walked down the steps of the police station he punched the air and grinned at Carly, sitting in the passenger seat of his car.

"Yes!" He opened the door and jumped in. "Their

investigations revealed fuck all! Jessie's been examined and there's nothing to find there either!" He kissed her, slightly out of breath. "I'm going to get absolutely wrecked; care to join me?"

"It's ten o'clock in the morning!" Carly laughed and returned his kiss. "But, hey, sure; let's stop off at the supermarket and load up on wine."

His mood was buoyant as he drove the few miles home. He felt as though a ton weight had been lifted from his shoulders which had been dragging him down for the past six weeks. As he unlocked the front door he placed the bottles of wine very carefully down in the hallway and took Carly in his arms.

"I'm as horny as hell; I thought I'd better let you know." He kissed her hungrily; his tongue mingling with hers which only added to his delicious frustration.

"Thanks for the info."

She unzipped his trousers and slid them down to the ground, together with his boxer shorts. As he stepped out of them he pushed her back against the stairs, lifting up her skirt and removing her panties.

"Have you ever had sex on the stairs before?" He moved her knees apart.

"No, 'cos it's too fucking uncomfortable." She laughed and braced her legs against the bannisters on either side.

"I'll be gentle." He whispered as he slid inside her.

He came to the conclusion that she looked like Aphrodite herself as she stretched out on the stairs, sexy and sated. He rose up from his kneeling position and feasted his eyes on her body, taking in the hitched-up skirt around her waist, and long bare legs leading up to a wonderful, deep, dark place that caused him to return there like a slave, time after glorious time.

"I can't get enough of you." He kissed her pubic mound and pulled on his boxers and trousers. "Can you help me out further? I now want to get as pissed as a newt. This day is turning out wonderfully." He winked at her as she sat up and rearranged her clothes.

"Bring it on; I'm happy to oblige." She buttoned up her blouse and ran her fingers through her hair. "Where's my panties?"

"Where you last left them, my darling."

"I didn't leave them anywhere; you ripped them off!"

He picked up her panties and waved them around in the air just as the doorbell rang. "Shit! Who's that?" He whispered.

"How the hell do I know? Give me my knickers!" Carly hissed. "Quick!"

With some effort he kept the grin from his face as he went to the front door and opened it, surprised and delighted at the sight before him.

"Boys! How lovely to see you!"

"Hey, Dad!" Tom stepped forward and gave his father a hug. "How's it going?"

"Good, thanks Tom. How's Jake?"

"Okay." Jake grinned.

Take your bikes around the back; I'll open the kitchen door."

With a quick glance at Carly to make sure she was dressed, Alistair closed the front door.

"Okay to meet the boys?" He ran a hand down the front of Carly's blouse.

"I thought we were going to get pissed?" She stuck out

her chest to greet his hand. "But I guess that'll have to wait? Am I presentable?"

"You're beautiful; they'll love you."

He followed her into the kitchen and opened the back door, grinning at his sons' expressions at the sight of Carly:

"May I present Tom and Jake?" Alistair looked at Carly and took her hand. "Boys, this is Carly."

"Hi boys; which one's which?" Carly smiled, well aware of the interest she was creating.

"I'm Tom, the more handsome one." Tom grinned.

"I'm Jake; he might be prettier, but he's thick."

"You both look mighty good to me." Carly laughed. "Jake, you look like your dad actually."

"Poor sod." Alistair let go of Carly's hand and ruffled Jake's hair. "Well, this is a surprise; we must make the most of it. Do you want anything to eat?"

"Is the Pope catholic?" Tom rubbed his hands together. "What have you got?"

"There's some roast pork left over from yesterday; fancy that in a sandwich with some apple sauce?"

"Now you're talking; we've only got spam fritters later on."

Alistair felt a painful stab of remorse shoot through him at his son's remark. He opened the fridge and took out a tub of margarine and a plate of pork slices wrapped in silver foil.

"I've put some money in the bank for Mum." He suddenly felt pleased to have done this, which went some way in helping to assuage his guilt.

"That's not what we've come here to ask." Tom glanced at Jake, who threw his brother a knowing look.

"Oh?" Alistair looked from one to the other. "What's going on then?"

"We'll come straight to the point.   Dad…. er…..can we come and live with you and Carly?" Tom searched his father's face for a change of expression. "We've found out from Mum what's been going on after we saw something in the local paper. We don't think it's fair; we're on your side."

Alistair paused mid-way between spreading margarine on a slice of bread, surprised beyond belief.

"Thanks for your show of support; it's awesome." He carried on with his task as though nothing had happened. "I didn't realise the Press had got hold of it. I'm soon going to be the talk of the county I expect." He fumed silently with anger, wishing he could get his hands on the person who had leaked the story. "However, this is Carly's house. I would need to discuss it with her before we come to a decision."

"Sure." Tom nodded. "We'll cycle round tomorrow when you've had a chance to talk about it later on. Not too much pickle on mine, please."

CHAPTER 30

"I'M SORRY ALI, but I'm not prepared to take on a ready-made family." Carly shook her head. "We'd never get any privacy. How can we have sex on the stairs with two hulking teenage boys walking around the house? Besides, I've only got two bedrooms; they'd have to share. They'd be next door in their room listening to every noise we made."

"It'd be difficult anyway; they're too far away from their school. The bus would never pick them up from here." He felt disappointed at her flat-out negative response, but hoped that she would settle for a compromise. "How would you feel if they stayed overnight on Saturdays for instance?"

"Sure; just not every Saturday. I'm sorry to put the dampers on it all, but I never wanted kids of my own, let alone someone else's." She shrugged. "I like my house to look the same when I come home from work as when I left. Kids just mess everything up."

"Hey; I understand. At least you're honest with me." He pulled the duvet up around them and took her into his arms. It was *me* who left them; I can't expect you to take two strangers into your house. You haven't even had a chance to get to know them properly yet."

"They seem like great boys, but…..sorry…." She sighed and snuggled up to him.

"Who the fuck leaked the story to the Press anyway?" He closed his eyes, still angry. "All the kids in the school will know about it now; my life won't be worth living."

"Hey, I'll sound it out on Monday when I go in, and see how the land lies." She kissed his cheek. "Don't worry; you're innocent. You've got nothing to be afraid of. Hold your head high and it'll soon blow over."

"I bet it was that prick on the governing body. What's his name….Rupert something or other. He never did like me. He probably got paid a fortune for that juicy bit of information."

"For all you know it could have been Ann or Jessie, upset at the police report. It's no use worrying about it; what's done is done." She gave him a squeeze. "I'll see if I can pick up on any gossip, but I'm not sure if Leonard has let it slip in the staff room that we're now living together. They might all clam up when they see me."

"I'm sick of this bloody village!" He sighed and sat up. "You can't do a fucking thing without somebody knowing about it. I bet the neighbours probably knew I was moving in even before I met you. The gossip's going to be all over the county by the end of next week!" He hugged his knees under the duvet and lowered his head down. "Do you fancy moving to London? We can make a fresh start; nobody will know anything about me there."

"Let's just see how things pan out when you're allowed back at work. You'll be moving over a hundred miles away from your kids if we go to London." She sat up and put her arm around him. "Plus the fact I'm a country girl; concrete and car fumes don't really do it for me."

"Nor me, but I'll put up with it if I can be anonymous again." He moved closer to her. "So shall we say to the boys that they can stay two weekends out of four every month?"

"Yeah, that sounds great." She kissed him. "It'll give me a chance to get used to them. It's a bit frightening having a ready-made family thrust on you!" She chuckled. "Who knows? I may like them so much I'll tell them to move in!"

"Ann'll probably go ballistic, but they're almost grown up now. I don't want to lose them. I know I've lost Jessie, but I've got to get used to it." He closed his eyes against the tears. "I loved her so much; she was my princess." He rested his elbows on his knees and sank his head down into his hands. "Why, why did she do something like that?"

"Don't forget Leonard offered to give you the number of a counsellor." She rubbed her hand up and down his back.

"I've got you; I don't need any counsellor." He rubbed his eyes with the palms of his hands. "I'll get through it; don't worry."

"You'll always have me, baby." Carly nibbled his earlobe. "I'm good at making you forget."

The letter plopped onto the doormat three days later. He was vacuuming the front room when he saw the postman open the garden gate. Switching off the cleaner he picked up the solitary envelope, noting the school's franked postmark. With a rapidly beating heart he read Leonard Carter's neat handwriting.

Dear Alistair,

At our meeting on 3rd September 2014 where I considered the need to suspend you from work as a consequence of the allegations that I had received, I write to confirm that following information passed to us by the police, myself and the governing body concluded that there was no case to answer.

I am now able to inform you that as your suspension has been terminated, you may return to school on the Monday morning after the October half term in order to meet with me in my office. The purpose of the meeting will be to discuss arrangements to facilitate the resumption of your normal duties, and any other issues of concern. If you wish, you may be accompanied by a workplace colleague or a representative of your trade union. It is unlikely to be possible to rearrange the date of the meeting if your chosen representative is not available.

Yours sincerely
Leonard Carter'

CHAPTER 31

AS HE WALKED back into the classroom for the first time on a bright morning in early November, he was touched by the welcome banner festooned across the blackboard behind his desk. He smiled as Adrienne Draper came up to him.

"Welcome back, Sir. We told Mr Carter that we wanted to come back to your tutor group!"

"Yeah!" Jack Denbigh's voice permeated the room. "We're all looking forward to another summer trip, especially as it'll be our last!"

"Thanks Denbigh; thanks Adrienne. I must say I'm very pleased to be back." Alistair suddenly felt like crying. "I'll just take registration before you go off to your lessons." He sat down with a sigh and picked up a pen, looking down at the register to hide his watering eyes.

"We knew you didn't do it Sir; you were in the newspaper, but I said to my mum that it was all lies." Adrienne held out a badly-wrapped box. "I saved my Alum Bay sand for you, Sir; it's in the shape of the Needles lighthouse."

"Thank you Adrienne." Alistair whispered as he took the box. "I'll keep it on my desk to remind me of the trip."

"Celie had better not puke if we go there again!"

Alistair, tears threatening to course down his cheeks, laughed as Kevin Sanderson managed to lighten the atmosphere from somewhere at the back of the classroom.

"Said in your own inimitable style, Sanderson." He tapped his pen on the table and looked over the heads. "I recognised your voice straight away."

"How did it go, tiger?" Carly was waiting for him in the car park.

"Not bad for a first day. I nearly bawled my eyes out when Adrienne Draper gave me her Alum Bay souvenir." Alistair pressed the button on his key ring to disable his car's central locking system. "So much for confidentiality; all the kids seem to know what's been going on." He sat down in the driver's seat, fastened his seat belt and switched on the engine.

"I've a good mind to complain; someone on the governing body's earned a lot of money from our misery." Carly opened the passenger door and sat down.

"Let it lie." Alistair shook his head. "The last thing I want is to stir it all up again. For all we know Ann could have contacted the Press after I told her to get a job."

"Did she?" Carly chuckled.

"Who knows? She still has the dinner lady job at St. Luke's I think, but in all reality she's going to find it tough to find anything else; she's been at home for eighteen years. I've been a real bastard of a husband to her." He exhaled, put the car in reverse, and backed out of the parking space.

"We couldn't help falling in love." Carly shrugged and clipped on her seat belt.

"I know that, and Ann and I were just coasting along anyway, but the guilt at what I've done to the family doesn't seem to be going away."

"How about what they've done to you? To falsely accuse you of something that threatens your livelihood is downright wicked!" Carly tossed her hair and looked across at him.

"I need to try and talk to Jessie and explain things. I don't know the best way to go about getting in touch with her." He drove out of the school gates and onto the main road.

"Have we got the boys this weekend?" Carly asked. "Perhaps you can railroad Tom into asking her whether she'd mind it if you phoned for a chat."

"It's an idea. I don't want to lose her. I'm prepared to forgive her for all the shit that's happened. She's my daughter; I still love her." He sighed. "She's part of me."

"That's very noble of you, but then again I've never had a daughter. You've obviously got a strong bond with her."

"I did have; I need to find out if it's still there. I hate to say this to you, but I'm not going to rest until I do."

The car picked up speed on the clear country roads. As he drove Alistair thought back to Jessie's warm little hand in his, the feel of her soft, silky hair, and the thrill of her voice saying *I love you, Daddy*. For the rest of the journey he was aware that Carly was remaining unusually silent, her lack of conversation continuing even as he pulled up on the driveway and applied the handbrake.

"Okay, darling?" He unclipped their seat belts and looked at her.

"Not really." She sighed and gazed straight ahead.

"What's wrong?" He moved one finger gently up and down her arm.

"I've had second thoughts, and maybe getting in touch with Jessie again is only going to end up in tears……yours." She sighed. "Let it rest; I don't think any good can come of it. She seems like a scheming little madam to me." Carly opened the passenger door and stepped out of the car. "Sounds like she's got it in for you anyway for leaving her."

Without waiting for an answer, Carly walked quickly to the front door and opened it. Alistair locked the car and followed her inside the house, aware of the sudden change in her mood. He had not noticed a mercurial pattern to her temperament before, and hoped the sudden frosty atmosphere might soon blow over. As she hung up her coat he stood behind her and put his arms around her waist.

"Hey, hey; what's going on? Have I suddenly fallen out of favour?" He lifted her hair and kissed the back of her neck.

"I just don't want to see you hurt again." She rested her arms on top of his. "It sounds like Jessie can wrap you around her little finger."

"No; I'm once bitten twice shy now. It would just be good if I can get back on speaking terms with her at least. She's been part of my life for thirteen years; I just can't turn my back on her."

"Well, on your own head be it." Carly wriggled free of his embrace. "Don't say I didn't warn you."

"Just you, Jake?" Alistair looked past his son into the front garden.

"Tom's gone down to Yarmouth with Clare." Jake shrugged. "I think he's in love."

"Take your bike around the back; I'll open the kitchen door." Alistair smiled at Jake.

"I didn't bring my bike; Mum brought me here in the car." Jake stepped into the hallway. "Hi Carly!"

"Hello Jake." Carly came out to greet him. "I think Dad's planned to take you out somewhere today."

"Great! Where are we going then?" Jake looked at Alistair with interest.

"Norwich are playing at home and I bought some tickets, but we can sell Tom's at Carrow Road unless you want to come with us Carly?"

"Oh God, no. I can't stand football. All those silly little men running around after a ball; it's pathetic." Carly wrinkled her nose.

"Er…. I guess it's just you and me then Dad?"   Jake chuckled.

"Looks like it." Alistair grinned. "I didn't realise Mum brought you. Is she picking you up tomorrow then?"

"No; she asked if you could bring me back."

"Sure; no problem." Alistair suddenly saw the opportunity he had been waiting for. "Any particular time?"

"Oh no, I think she's just glad to see the back of me."

CHAPTER 32

"THAT GOAL BY Wes Hoolahan was awesome! Thanks for taking me yesterday." Jake unclipped his seat belt and picked up his overnight bag.

"I've had a great weekend as well, Jake. Maybe Tom will be able to come over too in a fortnight?" Alistair ventured hopefully.

"Clare's giving him a bit of grief I think."

"Ah, yes; women tend to do that sometimes, son." Alistair gave a wry smile. "Do you think you can run in and ask your mum to come out here for a minute please?"

"Sure. See you soon, Dad."

"Bye, Jake."

He could see that Ann had appeared even before his son had reached the front door. He saw Jake speak to her briefly before running inside, and he climbed out of the car as she came towards him down the garden path, noticing her weight loss and a new improved shorter hairstyle.

"Thanks for having Jake this weekend; he just said he enjoyed the visit."

"That's okay; your hair looks different." He smiled at her.

"I've gone shorter and had some red highlights put in."

"It looks nice." He nodded. "Thanks."

"I'm glad I've had the chance to see you. I wanted to ask you if I could speak to Jessie please." He held his breath.

"Now?" She looked at him, puzzled.

"If possible. I just want to speak to her about everything and let her know I've forgiven her for the false accusations." He exhaled slowly. "Is she at home?"

"Yes, but……" Ann looked doubtful.

"Could you ask her if she'd see me, please?"

"Okay; hang on." She sighed. "Wait at the door and I'll speak to her."

It seemed strange waiting like a tradesman at his own front door. An eternity elapsed before Jessie appeared; she seemed to have grown taller over the last few months. He noticed a more womanly figure appearing, with the beginnings of a small bust.

"You've grown so much; I hardly recognised you." He smiled at his daughter, genuinely pleased that she had come down from her room to see him.

"What have you come to see me about?"

He thought that she seemed frightened, almost as though she wanted to run back to the safety of her room. Alistair took a step back so as not to alarm her further, aware that Ann would be listening just out of view.

"I just wanted to speak to you to explain about why I left home. I didn't get a chance to put my side of the story to you at the time, and so I'd like to do it now; hopefully not standing here on the doorstep though." He kept a smile on his face and shrugged. "It's cold, for a start."

"I'll ask Mum if you can come in."

As he stood there he noticed how the outside of the house needed a coat of paint. It had been five years since he had last painted the plasterwork, which was now showing definite signs of neglect compared to the neighbour's frontage. He looked behind him at the flowerbeds; the summer's growth of weeds had flourished, and a hardy type of convolvulus vine was gradually taking over.

As he turned back towards the half-open door, the sound of footsteps could be heard running along the hallway.

"Mum says it's okay."

He followed his daughter into the sitting room, which still looked the same except for a missing wedding photograph that had previously graced the wall above the chimney breast. Alistair sat down on the settee he had only just finished paying for six months previously, and noticed how Jessie curled up in the armchair furthest away from him. There was no sign of Ann or Jake, and so he smiled and grabbed the chance he had been given with both hands.

"What's happened to us, Jess?" He shook his head. "There's been so much hurt and anger, on both sides I must add. I had really wanted to talk to you before Mum told you that I was leaving, but I didn't get the chance." He sighed and maintained eye contact. "Can I put my side of the story to you now?"

"If you like." Jessie shrugged.

"There's no easy way to tell you that I fell in love with another woman. It just happened and there was nothing I could do about it. However, my feelings for you and the boys remain the same; I still love you just as much as I did before despite what's happened recently. I'd really like us to remain friends; the boys come and visit me as you know. I'd like for you to do that too. *I don't want to lose you, Jessie!*"

The last few words came out as a kind of pleading whisper. Alistair found himself leaning forwards on the settee, trying with all his might to elicit some sort of response from his daughter, who sat twisting a strand of hair around and around with her legs curled under her.

"You couldn't have loved me that much, otherwise you wouldn't have done what you did."

The flat, emotionless tone of her voice crushed him beyond belief. Alistair sank back on the settee and looked around the room in despair, remembering the times when he had sat on the floor with her playing Connect 4, a game she had taken a particular liking to before boybands had come on the scene. He could still see the game in its box on a dusty shelf underneath the TV.

"Do you recall how we used to play Connect 4? I taught you to play Chess, and how to swim. You used to sit on the back of my pushbike on that little seat and I'd take you for a ride. We had *fun*, Jess. Remember?"

"You used to wash me. I didn't want you to wash me." Jessie looked down at the floor. "You used to come into my room and shut the door and get on my bed. I didn't want you to do that."

"You were five, six or seven years old! What's got into you? Every Dad who loves his little daughter will give her a wash and read her a bedtime story!" Alistair shook his head. "You're getting things you've heard at school mixed up with what really happened. I would read you a bedtime story and kiss you goodnight. I'd been at work all day and hadn't seen you! That's all there was to it; nothing else."

"No." Jessie shook her head. "There was more to it and you *know* there was."

Alistair's heart thumped painfully in his chest at her words:

"*What* more? I don't know what you're talking about!"

"What about the game where I had to sit on your lap in my nightie?" Jessie held his gaze and uncurled her legs.

"That was the Eton rowing boat song. I used to hold your hands and we'd sway backwards and forwards and sing." Alistair shrugged. "The body between your knees song, I bet you can still sing it! Who's been filling your head with all this nonsense? It's one of the policemen who has done this, isn't it? He's put ideas in your head that shouldn't be there."

"I wasn't allowed to tell Mum about the song; it was our little secret you said. I only told her when you walked out."

"I thought a little innocent secret would help strengthen the bond that we had together" Alistair nodded. "You told Mum because you were angry that I'd left you."

"No; I told her because you were no longer here, I was free, and I wasn't frightened anymore."

"Pull the other one Jess! When were you ever frightened of me?" Alistair laughed. "This is madness!" He shook his head. "Somebody has really messed with your head!"

"Yeah, you did!" Jessie sneered at him. "I tried to tell the police, but you got away with it."

"Jessie; look at me. I'm your dad. We had a lot of good times; you must remember those?" Alistair, slightly panicked now, wracked his brain. "Who picked you up when you fell off your bike? Who stopped you from drowning in the swimming pool? Who played 'Schools' with you all weekend that time when you had a sore throat? I don't know how you could have said all the things you did! You know they're not true! The police told you that there was no evidence to charge me with anything!"

"The worst times were when Mum and the boys were out and I'd have to sit on your lap for a cuddle."

"Because you had that separation anxiety syndrome thing if Mum left you for even an hour. I'd try and comfort you." Alistair sighed. "Look; I came here to tell you that I love you and that you're always welcome to come and see me anytime. I just wanted you to know that." He stood up. "But by the sound of it you can't stand the sight of me. There's only a certain amount of time that I'll beg for your company, and that time has come to an end. I'll be going back I think; this whole thing is crazy. I hold out the faint hope that in time you might change the way you feel about me and want to keep in touch."

Aghast and near to tears, he made his way to the door of the sitting room, suddenly surprised at a mini tornado which had hurled itself forcefully against him:

"Don't go Daddy! Please don't go! I don't want you to leave!"

As Jessie flung her arms around him and sobbed, he heard Ann running from the kitchen. Alistair picked his daughter up like a baby, rocking her to and fro:

"Don't cry darling; Daddy loves you. I'll always love you; don't cry." He buried his face in her sweet-smelling hair. "Don't hate me; I love you."

"Don't leave me, Daddy! Please don't leave me!" Alistair, distraught and tearful, looked over Jessie's head at his wife, who appeared stricken at their daughter's outburst.

"Jessie, what's the matter?" Ann rushed forward. "Ali, what's going on?"

"I don't want Daddy to go!" Jessie sobbed. "Mum, please make him stay!"

"Daddy doesn't live here anymore, darling." Ann stroked Jessie's hair. "We have to get used to it."

Alistair carried Jessie to the settee, sat back down with her on his lap, wrapped his arms around her and rested his chin on the top of her head. Ann followed behind and took a seat next to him, sitting stiffly upright at an angle. For a while there was silence, broken only by the sounds of Jessie's sobs. When he could hear that his daughter no longer sounded distressed, Alistair gave her a gentle squeeze.

"Okay now?" He kissed the top of her head and ran the back of his hand over his eyes.

"Can you stay here tonight?" Jessie hiccupped. "Can he sleep here, Mum?"

"Dad will have to make that decision." Ann smiled at Jessie. "I'll leave it up to him."

"If it'll make you happy I'll sleep here tonight on the settee. How's that?" Alistair sighed with relief that Jessie had stopped crying. "We can even have a game of chess later on, just like we used to."

"I'm sorry, Daddy; sorry for what I did." Jessie sniffed and wiped her eyes with a tissue.

"You had every right to feel angry; you must have thought I'd abandoned you." Alistair gave her another squeeze. "I'd never do that."

"This is all my fault." Ann kept her gaze lowered. "I should have let you tell her first."

"It's too late now to go over who said what to whom and who did what." Alistair glanced sideways at Ann. "Let's forget it and take it from here. I'll pop back, have something to eat and a shower, and grab an overnight bag."

CHAPTER 33

"AND YOU AGREED to stay?" Carly looked at him incredulously. "Jeez, she's got you wrapped around her little finger!"

"She was absolutely distraught." Alistair put toiletries and some clean clothes into a rucksack. "I need to spend the evening with her and reassure her that I'm still her dad."

"I'm sure she already knows that." Carly sniffed. "Where will you be sleeping; in with Ann?"

"Don't be silly; I'll kip down on the settee and see you at the school."

"How will you manage it when she starts throwing another tantrum tomorrow as soon as you announce you're leaving again?" Carly threw him a pair of pyjama bottoms. "Here; you'll need these."

"It wasn't a show of temper." Alistair found Carly's lack of sympathy somewhat annoying. "Don't you think I can distinguish between a childish tantrum and genuine grief? I've brought her up for thirteen years for Pete's sake!" He packed the trousers and zipped up the rucksack with more force than was necessary.

"She's milking it. Next thing you know you'll be moving back in." Carly nodded to emphasise her point. "Ann will have suddenly lost a few pounds, will have had a new haircut and bought some flattering clothes, and you'll fall in love with her all over again."

"That's not going to happen." With alarm Alistair suddenly recalled Ann's slimmer figure and red highlights. "You've got it all wrong; it's just an overnight stay. Can I have a cuddle please, or am I in the doghouse?"

She came round the side of the bed towards him. "Of course you can have a cuddle." She put her arms around him. "You can have something else as well if you like."

"No time; got a few games of Chess to play." He kissed her. "Save it for tomorrow night."

"Hi Daddy! I've made you a bed; come and have a look!" He followed Jessie into the front room and nodded in approval at two pillows and a sheet and blankets folded neatly together on the settee.

"It looks very comfortable; I'm sure I'll sleep soundly tonight." He put his arm around her. "Thank you, darling."

"Can I sit on your bed and watch TV?" Jessie laughed.

"Sure; I'll sit with you." Alistair smiled at Ann and Jake, already seated in the armchairs. "What time can we expect Tom back?"

"Oh, he'll roll up about ten o'clock tonight. Terry will screech to a halt, and there'll be lots of honking of horns. God knows what the neighbours think." Ann rolled her eyes.

"He has to have a shower straight away, because he smells." Jessie wrinkled her nose daintily. "And he'll be really grumpy because he's so tired."

"Sounds like our boy is growing up fast." Alistair glanced at Ann. "Your turn next, Jake."

"I can't wait." Jake yawned. "It seems strange having you here again, Dad."

"It's just for tonight; I promised Jessie." Alistair gave his daughter a squeeze.

"You'll change your mind by tomorrow and want to move back in." Jessie nodded. "I just know it."

"Jessie, Mum and Dad are separated now; Dad lives with Carly." Jake shook his head at his sister. "You know that."

"No; he should be living here with us." Jessie inched closer to Alistair. "He's Dad; he belongs in *this* house."

"Jess, Jake's right; I can't live here with Mum anymore, but that doesn't mean that I don't love you. We've talked about this earlier." Alistair's heart began to thud at the thought of having to endure another scene.

"Why don't you love Mum?" Jessie sighed. "She still loves you; she told me."

"Jessie….." Ann blushed, looked at her daughter, and shook her head.

"We're a *family*, Dad!" Jessie exclaimed. "You, me, Mum and the boys."

"Family dynamics change, darling. In a few years you, Jake and Tom would have grown up, married and moved out. It's not fair if I live with Mum and stop her from finding somebody else to make her happy." Alistair kept his eyes averted from Ann and focused on Jessie.

"Mum doesn't want anybody else; she wants you."

Alistair felt the force of Jessie's stare and gazed down at the carpet. The silence was eventually broken by Jake, who reluctantly took his eyes away from the TV for the split second it took him to glance at his mother.

"If you want Dad to come back, why are you going out with Trevor then, Mum?"

The television continued blasting out a reality show with air-headed celebrities whom Alistair had never heard of, while the grandfather clock in the corner gave out its usual comforting tick. A pang of jealousy shot through him on hearing his wife uttering the words that to him seemed to hold a subtle underlying message.

"We're just friends."

He watched Ann's profile as she concentrated on the reality show; the new haircut suited her and she appeared younger. There were a few fine lines around her eyes and mouth, but as far as he could see she seemed to be holding up well for a woman soon to be forty one. Alistair's gaze travelled down her body; gone was the spare roll of fat around her middle, and her tight skirt emphasised a neat waist. Although he was aware that she could not hold a candle to Carly, he suddenly had a mental picture of a faceless man revelling in the sight of his wife's nakedness, and was unprepared for the feelings of anguish this image generated.

"Will I be in the way tonight?" He cleared his throat. "I mean.....will he.….?"

"He'll be round tomorrow." Ann crossed her legs and continued staring at the TV. "He's a landscape gardener; I originally advertised for somebody to dig over the flowerbeds. He's made a great difference to the back; go and have a look if you like."

He had to see the evidence for himself. Ruffling Jessie's hair he stood up, walked into the dining room, opened the back door and stepped out onto the patio. He almost gasped at the transformation. The box hedges he had planted so carefully to eclipse their view of the neighbours sunbathing had now been cut down to half their size. The earth in the flowerbeds had been turned over, and all the bushes and shrubs had been neatly trimmed. Alistair hid his anger as he heard footsteps behind him.

"He's done a grand job, although it's a shame the hedges have been cut down."

His anger turned to momentary sadness as he remembered all the hours he had spent teasing them into shape with the shears, pleased at the privacy they had afforded.

"They'll be easier to manage now they're not so high. I'll get the boys to cut them for some pocket money."

Her voice sounded matter-of fact and business-like. Alistair wondered if she remembered him putting his arms around her long ago on the same patio to stop her falling off a sun lounger they were both sharing, and how she had looked up at him with a self-satisfied smile and informed him she was eight weeks pregnant.

"*I* can always come round and cut them if you like."

He felt an indescribable melancholy seep through his core, spreading its tendrils into every fibre of his being. The house he had strived so long to pay for and own outright was now being maintained by another man, who by the sound of it was inching ever closer up the stairs towards the bedroom door; *his* bedroom door, with *his* slimmer and suddenly more attractive-looking wife.

"It would save money, sure." Ann shrugged. "But I like the hedges lower; I'm able to talk to Monica if she's out in the garden."

"You're too old for stories now." Alistair laughed. "But hopefully not too old for a kiss."

He sighed as Jessie threw her arms around his neck:

"I'll never be too old for that! Will you still be here in the morning?"

"Yes, and I'll run you to school; how's that?" He knew the journey would make him late for work, but to see the look on his daughter's face was priceless.

"Cool! See you in the morning, Daddy."

"Night, Princess."

Like hundreds of times before, he closed Jessie's door and popped his head into Jake's room.

"Don't sit too long at the computer."   He smiled at his son.

"I won't; it's strange having you back here." Jake looked around at him.

"It feels a bit peculiar for me as well. I'll wait up for Tom."

"He'll be in about ten." Jake turned back to the keyboard.

Alistair padded downstairs, unsure whether he should return to the sitting room or make himself scarce until his wife went up to bed. He elected to go into the kitchen and make a cup of tea. Switching on the kettle, he leaned against the work surface and waited for it to boil, noticing as he did so that the wall clock had stopped. He fished in the drawer behind him and took out two spare batteries at the same time as he heard Ann came into the room.

"I could never reach up there; thanks for that."She smiled at him. "The boys are either always too busy or out."

"That's okay; make the most of me if you need anything else doing."

"No, it's fine; just to be here for Jessie was a real help today."

"How does she get on with your boyfriend?" He held his breath as he filled up the teapot.

"It's early days, she hasn't got to know him yet; he's only seen her a few times when Mum was available to babysit. I don't like leaving her here on her own if the boys are out." Ann sat down at the table. "Everything back to normal at school now?"

"Yeah, mostly." He opened the cupboard and took out two mugs. "It's good that we can get along now."

"I think we're going to have to for Jessie's sake." Ann nodded. "Perhaps she and Jake can come over and stay with you one Saturday night soon so that Trevor and I can have a weekend together."

"Sure." Alistair's heart sank at the hidden implication of her words. "I'll talk to Carly."

"I'm going to bed now; actually I'll forego the tea. Goodnight." She stood up.

"I'll wait up for Tom; goodnight Ann." He poured himself a cup of tea and watched her retreating back with more than a touch of sadness.

CHAPTER 34

HE COULD NOT shake the sure and certain knowledge that he was now a guest in his own house. Alistair flicked through the TV channels, unable to concentrate or settle on any one programme. The grandfather clock, which had never bothered him before, ticked loudly and chimed every quarter of an hour, driving him to distraction. After he had changed into unfamiliar pyjamas he went over to the clock and disabled the pendulum, sighing with relief at the silence, and climbed onto the settee under the blankets. It was early; just gone ten o'clock, but as his son was due home any minute he decided to just lay there and wait for Tom's key in the door.

He must have dozed, for the next thing he knew somebody was shaking him awake. He sat up, trying to make sense of where he was while struggling with the handicap of a sleep-addled brain.

"Ali; wake up."

"What's wrong?" He looked at Ann, rubbed his eyes and yawned.

"Tom's not home. I've tried phoning him, but he's not answering his mobile."

Aware of his wife's tendency towards anxiety, Alistair kept an even tone to his voice, switched a lamp on nearby, and reached for his phone.

"It's only half past ten; he's not that late."

"He's never been this late before." She sat down at the end of the settee and looked at him helplessly.

He recognised her usual hint of panic. Alistair swung his legs down to the floor, stood up and went over to the window. The street was empty:

"Give him another half an hour or so; I'll try phoning him soon; it may be that he's in a place with no signal."

He pulled on a jumper over his pyjama top and sat down again beside her. She pulled her dressing gown more tightly around her and folded her arms:

"What have you done to the clock?" She looked towards the far corner of the room.

"I nobbled the pendulum; it was driving me mad." "Sorry to wake you up, but I'm worried."

"He's a young lad; there'll be many more nights like this one." He laughed ruefully. "My poor old mum never knew where I was; just as well really."

"He's discovered girls now, I think." Ann shrugged.

"Well, having sex will make him forget about coming home on time." He chuckled. "That's for sure."

"You should know." She gave him a painful smile. "Sorry…… that was a bit uncalled for."

He could have kicked himself. He shook his head: "No, I deserve that. I've been an absolute shit-bag." "Maybe if I'd been a bit more adventurous in the bedroom department you wouldn't have strayed in the first place." She leaned slightly forward, hugging herself. "Apart from the fibroids and the bleeding, I didn't think we had too much of a problem though until after I'd had the hysterectomy. Unfortunately I've never felt right since."

"You never said." He looked at her sharply. "Have you been to the doctor about it?"

"Funnily enough I only went after you left. He said it could be hormonal changes due to removal of the uterus, or nerve and blood vessel damage during the operation that are critical to sexual function, and which might take a long time to heal properly." She sighed and kept her eyes averted. "He'll only give me HRT when my ovaries start to fail."

"I'm sorry; I didn't realise." Alistair let out a shaky breath. "This makes me feel even more of a heel than I do already."

"You didn't know. It's not something I thought would happen to me while I was still relatively young; I thought it was a problem I'd face in about fifteen years." She gave a rueful laugh. "I've got menopause problems and I'm not even at *the change* yet. How unlucky am I?"

They watched an old film on TV that when questioned later, neither of them could remember anything about. As they sat in silence, each nursing their own thoughts but grateful for something to focus their gaze upon, the doorbell rang. Alistair jumped up.

"Here he is; he's forgotten his key." He pressed a button on the TV remote control to mute the sound.

"No; I never heard Terry's car; it's not Tom." Ann followed behind him.

He would always remember the sight of the policewoman's pale face in the moonlight. To Alistair it seemed as though she was standing there almost apologetically, embarrassed to be there. For several heartbeats they all stood looking at each other in silence until a voice Alistair realised was his started to speak.

"Can I help you?" His legs turned to jelly as he heard his wife gasp.

"Mr and Mrs Veale?" The policewoman made an effort at a genuine smile.

"Yes." Alistair spoke in unison with Ann.

"I'm WPC Sue Bishop; may I come in?"

He was aware that Ann had begun to cry. Alistair put his arm around her as he showed the policewoman into the sitting room. The TV was still on, and the flickering black and white images gave an eerie glow to the room, still only dimly-lit by lamplight. He held Ann close to him as he indicated an empty armchair.

"Please take a seat."

He sat back down on his settee-bed, with Ann clinging on to him for dear life. The policewoman cleared her throat and looked as though she wanted to be anywhere other than where she actually was at that precise time.

"I'm sorry to have to tell you this, but there has been an accident. A car driven by Mister Terence Fisher struck a tree headfirst at speed on the A47 this evening. Mr Fisher and Miss Alice Chandler, the front seat passenger, were not wearing seatbelts and were killed instantly. However, your son Thomas and another back seat passenger, Miss Clare Adams, both had their seatbelts fastened. They survived the crash. Your son is now in intensive care at the Norfolk and Norwich Hospital. Miss Adams was less injured; I think she's just being kept in on one of the wards overnight for observation."

"Jeez, no." Alistair whispered and clutched Ann tightly. The room swayed and reeled around him, and he closed his eyes. He sank his head down into Ann's hair, the lingering aroma of her shampoo he knew would bring back the horrific memory of that night for the rest of his life. He could tell that Ann was beyond words; shocked into a kind of stunned silence. He kissed the top of her head.

"Can we see our son, please?"

"Of course. I expect he will be in hospital for some time; A CT scan has confirmed dislocation of one of the cervical vertebrae. He also has swelling and bruising to the brain due to severe whiplash."

As if in a dream, he untangled his limbs from Ann's and stood up, picking his clothes up from the floor where he had thrown them only one relatively carefree hour before. With their son confirmed as being still alive, he was relieved to see that Ann had returned somewhat to a state of quasi-normality, although was still huddled tearfully on the settee.

"Ann, we must get dressed and make some phone calls." He reached out his hands to his wife. "Your mum will have to come over and stay with the kids."

"Yes, I'll phone her."

Her robotic voice as she stood up and took his hands caused him to pull her towards him and wrap his arms around her:

"He'll be okay, Ann; he's young and fit. He'll make it; don't worry."

"Will you be okay to drive to the hospital, Mr Veale?" WPC Bishop stood up, seemingly eager to depart.

"Yes; thank you for coming out and letting us know."

"I would like to say it's been a pleasure, but it hasn't." The policewoman grimaced and made her way to the front door. "I've done this so many times, and it never gets any easier."

CHAPTER 35

HE HAD TAKEN her hand automatically as they walked along eerily night-quiet corridors towards the Intensive Care Unit. The fact that she did not pull away and was happy to accept his support pleased him immensely. Alistair glanced down at his wife, resilient and stoical.

"Okay?" He squeezed her fingers.

"I will be once I've seen Tom."

The unit's entrance was key-coded. Alistair pressed the buzzer and announced themselves to a disembodied voice. As he pushed the door open his heart began to race in his chest, but he concentrated on comforting Ann, now crying silently, by putting an arm around her shoulder and holding her close to him. One of the night staff came up to the reception desk, while Alistair looked around in vain, trying to recognise which bandaged body lying prone and surrounded by tubes and monitors belonged to his son.

"Good evening; can I help you?"

The nurse smiled pleasantly, and Alistair suddenly felt

reassured that everything possible looked as though it was being done.

"We're Thomas Veale's parents. Can we see him please? We had a visit from the police earlier."

"Ah, yes. Mr Veale is in bed four." She indicated towards one corner of the ward. "We are keeping him sedated and ventilated in order to reduce the swelling and bruising to his brain. He is being fed through a naso-gastric tube. He has a rigid neck collar on to help reduce the cervical dislocation, and we'll perform another scan in a few days to assess any improvement. When the intra-cranial pressure has normalised we will lift the sedation. Also, if the collar does not reduce the dislocation, he may need surgery. However, he's stable and you can visit anytime. Try and keep talking to him if you can."

"Thank you."

Alistair, still with one arm around Ann, moved towards Tom. With horror he realised he could barely identify his son's swollen and lacerated features, which had been pushed further out of place by the stiff collar. Tubes, drips and monitors had seemingly taken over all his bodily functions.

Tears welled in the back of his eyes. Ann broke free from his grip and rushed towards Tom, silently picking up one of her son's hands while seating herself on a nearby chair. Alistair moved around the far side of the bed and took his other hand:

"Tom; it's Mum and Dad here." Alistair had no idea if the boy could hear him or not. "You're in hospital, but you're going to be okay."

He looked over at Ann, still crying noiselessly as she massaged Tom's fingers and wiped away falling tears with her other hand. He saw the digital time display on one of the monitors reading one thirty four. He looked around again; anywhere except at the barely recognisable face lying there so expressionless. Nobody except nursing staff flitted about, soundless and efficiently going about their business.

"If you can hear me Tom, squeeze my hand."

There was no pressure on his fingers. Alistair glanced over at Ann and shook his head:

"He's having a liquid cosh of course." He shrugged. "I expect we've just got to wait until they lift the sedation."

She nodded, numb to the bone. Resting Tom's hand gently back on the counterpane, Alistair lifted a spare chair from a stack by the wall, brought it over to the bed and sank down on it gratefully, rubbing his eyes.

"Thank God he's still alive." He let the tears fall and reached over to lay his hand on top of Ann and Tom's.

"He's so lucky." Ann nodded. "I feel for poor Terry's parents tonight, and those of the girl he was with."

"Young lads; it's a wonder any of them make it past adolescence." Alistair gave a shaky sigh. "Mother Nature shoots them full of testosterone and then leaves them to get on with it."

"You made it." Ann shrugged.

"Yeah, and look what it's done to me." He wiped his eyes. "The stuff should come with a Government health warning."

"That's why you were given a brain…..to control it."

"I make no excuses really; I fucked up." He liked how she kept her hand under his as he looked at her.

"Have you told her where you are?" Ann glanced away from his gaze towards Tom.

"No; I'll see her in the staff room anyway. I want to run Jessie to school because I promised. If we go in a while I'll grab an hour's sleep, have a shower, take Jessie, and then go to work."

"You won't be fit to teach today." Ann shook her head.

"I've had too much time off already. I'll cope."

He knew she would be waiting for him in the car park. Alistair turned off the engine, yawned, and waved as she ran towards him and opened the driver's door.

"Hey tiger, you look like shit!"

"Cheers; I've been up all night at the Norfolk and Norwich."

"What? Why? What's happened? Why didn't you phone me?"

Her questions came thick and fast. Alistair did not think he could relate all of the previous night's happenings without crying. Instead he held up the palm of his hand as a sign of submission, locked the car, and shook his head.

"It's Tom, but later; I can't do it now. I need to go back this evening and see him."

"Oh; I'm so sorry, darling. I'll come with you."

"No, best not; Ann will be there."

"God, sorry. I forgot." Carly thumped her forehead with a fist.

"It's okay; I'll definitely be home sometime this evening though." He yawned again and hoped against hope that he could keep awake.

There were no staff he recognised from the night before as he passed by the reception desk. He could see that Ann was already seated by the bed, holding Tom's hand and staring into the distance. Alistair walked slowly into her line of vision so as not to startle her, and was rewarded with a thin smile.

"Hi; have you been sitting here long?" He returned her smile, pulled the spare chair nearer the bed, and took Tom's other hand in his.

"I drove up after work; I've been here since about half past two. His girlfriend came in with her mum, but left after a while; she was too upset to see him like this."

"Any change?" He looked at his son's face for any sign of improvement, but could see none.

"They're going to scan him again tomorrow. We won't know anything until then." Ann stroked Tom's hair and spoke near to his face. "It's Mum. Squeeze my fingers if you can hear me."

"Who's sitting with the kids?"

Alistair could tell by the expression on his wife's face that there had been no response from Tom. Shaking her head, she looked at him:

"Mum picked them up from school. I'll go back about eight o'clock and get them. I don't think it's a good idea for them to see Tom yet."

Bone-achingly weary, Alistair nodded and intertwined Tom's warm fingers with his own. All around him was a kind of unhurried efficiency. A nurse came over to check monitors and change the drip bags, and smiled at them briefly.

"He's doing fine."

A silence had settled over them while the nurse had gone about her business. After she departed Alistair glanced over at his wife, noticing the lines of worry and tiredness etched on her face."

"If you want to go now and get some sleep, I'll sit with him."

"No, I'll stay; you look as knackered as I feel."

"I've had better days; I've had better years come to that."
He shook his head. "God; how have we come to this? I laid
on the settee last night and realised I'm a guest in my own
house."

"You made a choice, Ali. You chose Carly." Ann
shrugged and looked away.

"I'm so fucked up at the moment I don't know what I
want." He leaned forward on the chair and rested his head on
the bed. "But I do know something. I love my kids; I'd go to
the ends of the earth for them. You deserve better than me;
you've got Trevor now and good luck to you……"

His voice trailed off as he fell asleep almost immediately,
still holding his son's hand.

A delicious aroma of coffee assailed his senses as he opened
his eyes and realised with embarrassment that he must have
dozed off. He sat up in alarm and looked at the time on the
monitor; seven twenty three. Ann was standing over him
holding a steaming cup.

"I thought you might like this. It'll wake you up a bit
before you have to drive home."

"Thanks." He took the cup from her outstretched hand.
"Some devoted father I am; hope I wasn't snoring."

"You were, but then again you always do."

He took a few welcome sips and checked on Tom. No
movement of his limbs, although the steady rise and fall of
his chest was reassuring. Alistair stood up, feeling a little
better for his impromptu sleep.

"Yeah, I'll have to get back soon. Perhaps tomorrow
there might be some improvement." He yawned and looked
at Tom again. "Promise I won't fall asleep tomorrow, son."

"Someone's got to tell him that Terry's dead." Ann sighed.

"I'll do it when he's strong enough to take it." Alistair drained the cup. "One step at a time."

CHAPTER 36

HE COULD SEE that she had already drawn the curtains in the sitting room against the chilly November night as Alistair parked the car outside Carly's house. As he walked up the garden path he took the key out of his pocket and fingered its unfamiliar lines and grooves, still a little sleepy and confused at his ambivalent feelings towards his change in circumstances. When he approached the house the front door flew open and a kind of red-headed whirling dervish threw herself at him in the porch.

"Oh, I'm so glad you're home! How's Tom?" She kissed his lips, his cheeks, and his neck. "I've missed you so much! My bed's too cold without you!"

"No change in Tom; they're going to scan him again tomorrow."

He put his arm around her and led her in to the hallway out of sight of the neighbours. As the front door closed he put both arms around her and sank his face into the warmth of her neck.

"Hello darling, I've missed you too." He chuckled,

unprepared for the ferocity of her greeting. "I only saw you in the staff room a few hours ago."

"But I couldn't touch you." She whispered, running her hands up and down his back. "All I've been wanting to do is cuddle you and tell you I've been hoping and praying that Tom's going to be alright."

"I'm sure he will be; it's just a matter of waiting." He closed his eyes and breathed in the scent of her. "I'm so bushed I fell asleep on his bed tonight."

"Oh you poor darling." She ushered him towards the kitchen. "Dinner, shower and bed for Sir is the order of the evening."

"Sorry to be a party pooper, but I think you're right." He shook his head. "I'm not sure I can even stay awake long enough to eat anything.

He let himself enjoy her pampering. Later, as he sank gratefully into bed onto the warm, soft pillow of her breasts, he fell unconscious and remembered nothing more until the shrill ringing of the alarm clock at six thirty the next morning.

He could not shake the depressing feeling that sometimes he felt he was in the wrong house. Carly was uncommunicative first thing in the morning; Jessie and Ann were talkative. The boys would just grunt until they had eaten something, but he could sit and chat animatedly with Jessie or Ann at the breakfast table over their bowls of cornflakes, no matter what the time. He had recently come to the conclusion that he missed the early morning interaction.

Carly slipped out of bed naked, then yawned and stretched. Under the sheets he enjoyed the feel of an erection at the sight of her body. As she threw on a robe he turned over on his front to try and block out the image of her full breasts and delightfully pert nipples.

"Don't even think about it, tiger." She fished around for her slippers, yawned again, and padded towards the door.

Grinning, he levered himself up on one elbow and reached for his phone. By the look of it, Ann was up already:

'Jessie wants to know when she can see you again.'

He felt a little thrill of pleasure shoot through him. He sat up in bed and tapped in a brief reply:

'Will discuss at the hospital tonight. See you later.'

The fact that his daughter was not lost to him was enough to make him jump out of bed, quickly pull on a pair of boxers, and bound lightly down the stairs to join Carly in the kitchen, who sat staring into space nursing a cup of coffee.

"Jessie wants to see me again; that's great isn't it?" He smiled and grabbed a mug.

"Yeah." She sipped some coffee, yawned, and then drank some more.

"Try and control your enthusiasm." He poured some still-hot water out of the kettle into a mug and added some coffee. "I always get the feeling you don't like her."

"Look; it's half six in the morning. I don't do talking until after my second cup of coffee; you know that." Carly put her mug down on the table a little too forcefully. "All I'll say is although I've never met her it seems that she's got you exactly where she wants you."

"Which is?" He topped up the mug with a dash of milk.

"As I've said before; around her little finger." "Don't be stupid; she's just a kid." He sighed.

"A very manipulative one. She'll split us up; you know that, don't you?" Carly looked at him. "She piles on the guilt, and you go running. She's got you by the short and curlies."

His happy *my-daughter-wants-me-and-my-son-is-going-to-live* mood suddenly evaporated. He drained his mug and stood up:

"They're my kids; I'm not going to turn my back on them."

"And where does that leave me?" Carly shrugged. "I'm not prepared to play second fiddle. If I can't be the most important person in your life, then you'd best go home."

"Ann's got Trevor now." He held the palms of his hands up towards her. "Hey! What's wrong with you this morning? I love you; isn't that enough? Can't a father love his kids as well?"

"They're not *my* kids. Every time I see them I think of you having sex with Ann."

"Now you *are* being unreasonable! After school I'm going to the hospital to see how my son is. My wife will be there as well; the one I used to have sex with. I'll tell you what; if there's a spare bed next to Tom I'll ask her if she'd like to have sex with me again while we're waiting for him to wake up! How's that?"

He walked out of the kitchen and slammed the door. He ran back up the stairs, grabbed some clothes and went into the bathroom, throwing open the door to the shower and not caring as it hit the wall with a loud thud before banging shut. Turning up the dial, he stood underneath the hot jet of water, letting the spray hit his face and wash away his rage. As he stood there he heard the door open with a small squeak, and felt wet arms slide around his waist.

"Sorry; you know I'm really cranky in the mornings."

He turned around and let the spray pummel his back while he took Carly in his arms:

"I'm sorry too; you *are* important to me, but so are my

kids. I love you so much. Stick with me while I try and sort everything out in my head."

He kissed her, running his hands over her breasts. As he felt her respond he grew hard and kissed her more passionately, sliding his tongue around hers and enjoying the feel of her fingers retracting his foreskin. As he lifted her up against the shower wall she kissed him again and moaned slightly, wrapping her legs around his hips.

"I love you; you're my world." He slid inside her, closing his eyes and throwing back his head in ecstasy.

"I love you too." She whispered, nibbling and sucking his neck. "Don't go; don't ever leave me."

CHAPTER 37

HE WATCHED AS the nurse took another set of observations. When she finished she turned towards them and raised her thumb.

"The intra-cranial pressure is coming down nicely. His blood pressure and oxygen levels are good. We'll be able to lift the sedation and take him off the ventilator hopefully next week. We don't like to leave them on ventilators too long if we can help it, as there's always the chance of pneumonia. He's doing really well though."

Alistair looked at Ann and smiled, receiving an answering grin. He tried to remember the last time he had smiled at his wife, but could not.

"That's great news!" He nodded. "Do you think Tom will remember anything of the accident?"

"Most unlikely. Most if not all patients have amnesia or some sort of memory problems after this type of injury. We'll have to see how he goes." The nurse wrote down the observation results in a chart clipped to the end of the bed. "I'll leave you for now, but I'll be back in an hour to take more obs."

He turned from Ann towards Tom, still lying prone and unresponsive:

"Did you hear that, Tom? They're going to lift your sedation soon." He squeezed his son's hand. "You'll be back at college in no time at all."

"Clare came in to see you." Ann took Tom's other hand. "She's a nice girl."

A silence settled over them as they both tried to think of something else to say. Finally Alistair checked his phone; the last message from his wife was still displayed on the screen.

"Thanks for your text this morning. I can take Jessie and Jake out somewhere at the weekend if you like."

"That'll be fine. Will they stay at yours overnight?" Ann looked up at him questioningly.

"Er….best not at the moment." He suddenly had a mental picture of Carly's expression at the breakfast table. "If you and Trevor want to go out I can sit with them until you get home."

"Trevor's just doing the gardening actually. I went out with him only the once for a drink, but I realised that he's not my type. Silly really; who at the end of the day is going to be interested in a forty year old woman with three kids?" Ann shrugged and gave a wry laugh. "It's a bit embarrassing now when he comes round, although the kids seem to like him."

"You're an attractive woman." Alistair felt a surprising amount of relief at her words. "Don't let anybody tell you any different."

"I'm a poor show compared to Carly, but then most women are." Ann nodded. "I can see why you're attracted to her."

"I'm sorry, Ann. I fell hook, line and sinker for her. She's hateful in the mornings though." He chuckled. "It's not all good."

"No relationship ever is." She looked away from him. "I'm sorry too; Jessie and I put you through hell."

"It's over now; I want us to remain friends. Hell, I care what happens to you and the kids, whatever's gone on in the past." He reached across the bed with his other hand. "We were married nearly twenty years for God's sake!"

"We're *still* married, Ali." Ann placed her hand on top of his. "Had you forgotten?"

"No, of course not."

"What do you want to do about that?" She glanced quickly at him. "I can file for divorce on the grounds of your adultery. It'll be all over in a few months."

"Whatever you want." He nodded. "It's not fair on you otherwise. Of course you need to be free to find somebody else."

"I don't know if I ever will, but I need to be given the chance."

"Sure; go ahead." He felt a sudden all-encompassing sadness. "I'll agree to anything you like"

He was certain there was something eerie about hospital corridors at night. Resisting the urge to put an arm around his wife, Alistair walked as close to her as he could get away with. He smiled at Ann as she turned to look up at him.

"I'm going to put in for that teaching assistant vacancy. Jeanie Lovell's announced she's not coming back after her maternity leave finishes at Christmas."

"That's great; I'm sure you'll get it." Alistair nodded. "It'll be a good step up for you."

"Yes, what with Jessie at the upper school now, I've got more time on my hands."

"I'm really pleased for you, and I'm happy that we can

remain friends." He took her hand almost unthinkingly. "I'll be round on Saturday afternoon to take the kids out, if that's alright by you."

"Fine; you can stay to dinner afterwards if you like."

He was pleased that she did not automatically try to pull away. He was conscious of the pleasurable feeling it gave him to be able to walk along holding his wife's hand, as indeed he had done so for as long as he could remember. They walked the rest of the way to the multi-storey car park in silence, each immersed in their own thoughts. As they neared the lifts, he came out of his reverie.

"What level are you on?"

"Two."

"I'm on six. I guess we'll say goodbye until tomorrow then."

"Goodbye, Ali. Let me know about dinner on Saturday."

"Will do."

It seemed the most natural thing in the world to bend forwards and brush her lips with his own:

"Our son's going to be alright." He kissed her and put his arms around her. "Look after yourself, Ann."

"I will." She nestled her head against his shoulder and wrapped her arms around his waist. "Why do you always smell like shower gel?"

"At least it's better than B.O." He laughed. "Oh, Annie, Annie, what have we done?" He exhaled slowly into her hair.

"We became too complacent and let each other slip away." She sighed. "I stopped showing you affection; no wonder you strayed. It was as much my fault as yours."

"It feels so right holding you like this." He kissed the top of her head.

"You need to go home to Carly now." She broke away, and pressed the button for the lift. "I'll see you tomorrow."

The lift was already on the ground floor, and they stepped inside. Alistair pressed levels two and six, and without complaint from Ann, put his arms around her again.

"I owe you one more kiss to show I'm not mad at you."

He kissed her open mouth as he had done so many times before in the past, sliding his tongue across to mingle hungrily with hers. He was surprised at the force of her response. When the lift doors opened she disentangled herself from his embrace and smiled.

"I know you're not mad at me."

She stepped out of the lift and waved, before disappearing from sight as the doors closed once again, leaving him stunned, confused, and ever so slightly bereft.

As soon as he saw Carly curled up on the settee watching TV and crying, he ran to her. She smiled through her tears and cuddled up to him.

"What rubbish are you watching?" He laughed and ruffled her thick curls, smelling vaguely of coconut and taking him back to those first heady days on the Isle of Wight.

"It's a film with Meryl Streep; I like her films. She loved Denys Finch Hatton so much, but they've just buried him." Carly wiped her eyes and pressed the pause button on the remote control. "How's Tom?"

"Improving; they're going to think about lifting the sedation after the weekend."

"Oh, that's great!" She kissed him. "Your dinner's in the microwave; two minutes on full."

"Thanks." He slipped a hand inside her robe and

fondled her breast. "You're too good to me."

"Bugger off, I'm really into this film now." She tied her robe up tighter. "Go and eat your dinner."

Laughing, he stood up and went into the kitchen and turned on the microwave, sitting down at the table while he waited, with thoughts jumbling about incessantly inside his head.

He loved two women, of that he was sure, and loved them more every time he saw them. But how could he resolve the current desperate situation?

When the microwave pinged he took out his dinner and fetched a knife and fork from the drawer. He ate mechanically, hardly even noticing what food there was on the plate.

Was he yearning to return to Ann and the house he had strove so hard to pay for and the children he loved more than life? Should he stay with Carly, the most beautiful woman in the world? Could he live without the passionate sex he had with Carly if he went back to Ann? Would Carly eventually turn into Ann ten years down the line? Why the fuck had he been so stupid and got himself into this situation in the first place?

As he chewed he thought to himself that what he really needed was to get absolutely shit-faced crawling-into-your-shoe drunk. In that way he would not need to think about his dilemma, his injured son, or the fact that he was running a home he did not live in anymore. He nodded to himself, got up from the table and took a bottle of wine out of the fridge, intending to make substantial inroads on his quest. He uncorked the bottle and took a swig, dispensing with the nicety of using one of Carly's lead crystal glasses.

"What are you doing?

He was aware that Carly had come into the kitchen and

was eyeing him up and down suspiciously.

"Getting pissed; it's going to be a long job though." He took another long drink from the bottle.

"What's up, tiger?" She came and put her arms around him. "It's Friday tomorrow and you can't teach with a hangover. Save it for tomorrow night and I'll join you." She chuckled and rubbed her body against him.

"I'm just a total and utter cock." He sighed and took another swig.

"Bollocks. You really are talking bollocks." She took the bottle out of his hand. "Give me some of that; you sound like you've had too much already."

"I love you." He undid her robe and slid his hands around her waist to her bare back.

"I love you too. What's got into you tonight? Is it Tom?" She looked up at him.

"No, it's me; I hate myself."

"Well, have a shower and then come and hate yourself in bed. I'll see what I can do about it." She unbuttoned his shirt and rubbed her nose in his chest. "Hmm; male pheromones."

CHAPTER 38

HE SMILED AS soon as he saw the back of Ann's head as she leaned over and spoke to Tom. Alistair approached the bed noiselessly and ruffled her hair, noticing for the first time how much the texture of it differed from Carly's luxurious tresses.

"How's he doing?" He pecked her cheek and looked over at his son.

"Okay, I think. The nurses are pleased with his progress." She smiled up at him. "Intra-cranial pressure is normal. They've started to lift the sedation. He's breathing on his own now as you can see."

"Wow! That's good news!" Alistair sat on the side of the bed next to Ann and took Tom's hand. "Tom, I hadn't noticed your ventilator had gone. You're doing absolutely fine." He applied some pressure to the hand. "Squeeze my fingers if you can hear me."

"I've already tried that; there's no response yet." Ann shook her head. "They're lifting it slowly. Perhaps he'll be a bit more awake by tomorrow." She smoothed Tom's hair. "I was thinking of bringing Jake and Jessie in to see him soon."

"Good idea. I've got them over the weekend haven't I?" Alistair noticed how his wife's hair shone under the harsh ward lighting. "I'll bring them in to see him tomorrow evening maybe."

"Or Sunday morning; he might be a bit more awake by then." Ann nodded.

He could see that she looked somehow different, but could not for the life of him work out exactly why. Eventually he took a breath and decided to ask.

"You're looking nice." He scanned every inch of her face. "Have you used different make-up or something?"

"Ha ha! That's where you're wrong." She waggled a finger at him playfully. "I'm not wearing any make-up at all; just moisturiser."

"Really? You should do that more often; I like it." He realised at the same time how Carly never wore make-up either. "It takes years off you."

"Thanks. Something needs to; I'm forty one next year."

"I like the natural look. Those women with orange faces and tidemarks around their necks look hideous." He laughed. "Especially the ones with the trout pouts as well."

"No, I won't be getting a trout pout." Ann giggled. "You can rest assured on that one."

"I like it when you laugh." He sighed and took her hand. "It sounds like water trickling over stones."

"Oh God, don't get all poetic on me. Have you been doing Byron or Shelley at school today by the merest chance?" Her eyes glittered with mirth.

"How did you guess?" He caressed her fingers.

"You always did come home a bit other-worldly when you were teaching poetry."

"I feel like writing it sometimes." He squeezed Tom's hand again. "Hey Tom, would you like your old dad to write you a poem?"

The warm fingers remained still. Alistair, disappointed, looked at Ann and smiled:

"Never mind; it's probably best that I don't." He grimaced. "Lord Byron I'm not."

"I don't know about that." She giggled again. "I've still got that one you wrote me when we were first married."

"Yeah?" He looked at her in surprise. "I can't even remember writing it now, let alone what I said."

"Something about how I was very neat and clean." Ann kept a straight face. "Remember what came after that?"

"Oh God, yes I do!" He burst out laughing. "I didn't realise you would keep it all these years."

"It's in my memory box with the kids' teeth and baby hair."

"Don't let them see it."

"It's locked."

"Ah."

They looked at each other and smiled.

"What level are you on tonight?" He kept hold of her fingers with one hand, and pressed the button to call the lift with the other.

"Five. I got here a bit later."

"Same as me. We can drive out together then. I don't like you walking around these places at night on your own."

As they stepped into the lift it seemed only natural for him to take her into his arms. Her slimmer body felt fragile and delicate; smaller than Carly's. He wanted to protect her from all the Trevors of the world; shysters only keen on chancing their luck at getting into her pants.

"It feels good to hold you." He sighed.

He kept one arm around her shoulder as the lift door opened at level five. Apart from their own cars, only four others were parked. Keeping Ann close to him, Alistair looked for her car and walked towards it, coming to a halt by the driver's door. He wrapped his arms around her and rested his chin on the top of her head:

"I'm basically a bastard, but I've never stopped loving you. We go back a long way; you're my wife and the mother of my kids. Whatever you want, just name it."

"I want you to come home." She sobbed into his chest. "The house isn't the same without you in it."

He lifted her chin and kissed away her tears.

"You've got it. I'll come home to you baby, just as soon as I can."

He could not focus on her properly as she stood at the front door; his body seemingly not able to obey his commands. The whole scenario suddenly appeared hilarious to him, and he burst out laughing.

"Jeez! Have you driven home in that state?"

He held his hand out to Carly as he staggered up the garden path, loosely clutching the remnants of the second bottle of cheap wine which fell out of his hand and dropped with a crash onto the path, smashing into shards and smithereens. Before reaching the front door his stomach lurched uncontrollably, and he vomited the contents of both bottles into the flowerbed.

"Fucking hell! You can stay out there in the bloody garden until you've sobered up!"

He heard the door slam, and laughed again. In the distance he could hear the church clock, but could not seem to count how many chimes there were. Somewhere about his person he knew there would be a bunch of keys, but the effort of searching for them was too much for him at that precise moment.

The street was quiet. Overhead an owl hooted and flew past, eerily pale against the night sky. Alistair looked up to watch it, then reached out and tried to touch the snowy white feathers. As he did so his precarious balance was further compromised and he fell gracelessly down onto the path, landing with a smile on the shattered glass of the wine bottle.

CHAPTER 39

THE MOTHER OF all headaches hit him as he came to in the now familiar black-walled bedroom. As he opened his eyes he saw her sitting on a chair and looking at him with eyes seemingly devoid of any emotion.

"Feel better now you've slept it

off?" He shook his head.

"No."

"It serves you right. I had to get Billy next door to help me get you upstairs."

"Sorry. I'm just a fuck-up." He struggled to rise. "Any coffee?"

"Perhaps your wife will make you some."

He searched through the fog of his brain and wondered why Ann was downstairs in Carly's kitchen.

"Is she here then?"

"No. She's at home; where *you* ought to be."

He sank back onto the pillows with a sigh.

"So sorry."

"All the time you were out of it you were muttering her

name. Ali, no woman wants to be second best, and that includes me. You need to go home to Ann, and I need to find a man who isn't torn between me and somebody else. You're doing my head in. I'll make you some coffee, but it's over, Ali. I've had enough of coming in second to your wife."

He watched her as she stood up. He had never seen a woman so beautiful, but as she walked out of the room he knew she was right. The best sex in the whole of East Anglia wasn't enough; he had commitments to his wife and children. Tom would need him until he was back on his feet, and he needed to work harder to build up his relationship with Jessie and Jake again, which had taken a back seat to his own selfish desires. Alistair stared up at the ceiling and wished that he could turn back the clock.

At the sound of her footsteps on the stairs he gingerly swung his legs over the side of the bed and slowly assumed a kind of sitting/slouching position. He looked down at his arms, which were covered in cuts and scratches, and then up at Carly as he took the welcome hot drink from her hands.

"You fell on some glass."

"All the stress made me decide to get absolutely rat-arsed." He took a sip of coffee. "I should have stayed sober and sorted the whole sorry mess out."

"But you didn't." Carly nodded. "Me and Billy had to carry you up here instead. If you're wondering who took your trousers off, it was Billy."

Alistair looked down at his bare legs as though seeing them for the first time.

"At least he left my pants on."

"Let's be grateful for small mercies." He tried to force a grin.

"It's not *that* small."

Carly rolled her eyes heavenwards.

"Whatever size it is, it stays there in your pants. Once you've had a shower and tidied yourself up, you need to go home, Ali."

"I know, I know." He nodded. "But what will you do? Will you stay on at the school?"

She shook her head.

"I was mulling over things a lot last night while you were out of it. I realised I'd quite like to move to the Island and teach in one of the schools there. Thinking about that trip we had has made up my mind for me."

Alistair looked at her in surprise.

"You'd be welcome to stay in our house in Ventnor if you like, until you sort out a place of your own."

The smile he received was genuinely warm.

"Cheers for that Ali; it wouldn't be for long. Once I've found a job and seen a house I like, then I'll go for it."

"I'm sure you will." Alistair sighed. "We were good together, weren't we?"

Carly gave him a quizzical look.

"The sex? Yeah, it'll be hard to find somebody to fill your shoes, pardon the pun."

"No, not just the sex." He shrugged. "I *do* love you for God's sake, it's just that I found Ann first. We had children, three of them, and that complicates things as far as I'm concerned."

"*We* just happened." Carly nodded. "We were in the right time and the right place. We didn't think of the consequences, at least *I* didn't."

"Neither did I." Alistair admitted. "I took one look at you and that was it."

He watched Carly's eyes misting over, and took one of her hands in his. She leaned over and kissed his forehead.

"I'll give a term's notice, and then I'm going over to the Island. All I know is that if I ever do find somebody to settle down with, I absolutely know they couldn't hold a candle to you. Just thought I'd tell you that."

"I'm just a loser of the highest order." Alistair shook his head and blinked back tears. "There's millions of blokes out there just champing at the bit to get to know you. You deserve better than me."

"Piss off and have a shower and a shave then. Don't turn up on your own doorstep looking like you've been run over."

As he stepped out of the shower he felt a surge of relief, coupled with a pang of regret. He knew that going home was the right thing to do, but in all his 42 years he had never found the excitement of an ideal sexual partner until he had met Carly. He finished dressing and then idly picked up her bottle of shampoo that she had left on the side of the bath. Opening the lid, he put his nose to the top of the bottle and took a deep breath in. *Coconut.* He wondered whether he could ever smell coconut shampoo again without thinking of her.

She was waiting for him in the hallway. Alistair, head thumping in time to his heartbeat, walked heavily down the stairs and tried to keep his gaze fixed on the front door, but found that his eyes automatically sought hers. When he reached the bottom of the stairwell she threw herself into his arms and pressed her face into his shoulder.

"So long, tiger."

Her voice was muffled and full of emotion. Alistair

wrapped his arms around her, closed his eyes, and buried his face in her hair.

"I'll try and stay away from the staff room. I'm just a weak bastard."

"Me too; it's why I need to go."

He cupped her chin and lifted her face up to meet his.

"I love you; don't you ever forget that."

She laughed and wiped away a river of tears.

"I know, but I fucking *hate* you."

He let his lips brush against her forehead.

"I wish I could stop the clocks."

She smiled.

"Just give me one more kiss."

When his lips met hers he knew that for as long as he lived he would never feel such passion again for another human being. He wanted to drown in her there and then.

"See you in the playground."

"Not if I see you first."

He ran a hand through her curls, savouring their texture for the last time, and then picked up his car keys from the hall table. Without another word he opened the front door and walked away.

THE END

If you have enjoyed this story, you may also like *The Donor*.

OTHER BOOKS BY STEVIE TURNER:

The Pilates Class
A House Without Windows
No Sex Please, I'm Menopausal!
Lily: A Short Story
For the Sake of a Child
Cruising Danger
A Rather Unusual Romance
The Daughter-in-law Syndrome
The Noise Effect
The Donor
Repent at Leisure
Life: 18 Short Stories
Waiting in the Wings
Mind Games
Leg-less and Chalaza
A Marriage of Convenience

www.ingramcontent.com/pod-product-compliance
Lightning Source LLC
Chambersburg PA
CBHW070454200726
48293CB00007B/2196